THE GIRL HUNTERS

Doll Winters was a naïve teenager, who fantasised about being a film character. But when Gerald Dodd committed a brutal killing, she found herself starring in a real-life murder drama — as the star witness! And when Dodd tries to silence her, Doll turns for help to the famous private detective Simon Brand. Then a further terrifying attempt on her life forces her to go on the run. But can Brand find her before the killer can?

SYDNEY J. BOUNDS

THE GIRL HUNTERS

Complete and Unabridged

LINFORD
Leicester

First published in Great Britain

First Linford Edition
published 2006

British Library CIP Data

Bounds, Sydney J.
    The girl hunters.—Large print ed.—
    Linford mystery library
    1.Witnesses—Fiction
    2.Trials (Murder)—Fiction
    3. Detective and mystery stories
    4. Large type books
    I. Title
    823.9'14 [F]

    ISBN 1–84617–415–5

Published by
F. A. Thorpe (Publishing)
Anstey, Leicestershire

Set by Words & Graphics Ltd.
Anstey, Leicestershire
Printed and bound in Great Britain by
T. J. International Ltd., Padstow, Cornwall

This book is printed on acid-free paper

1

Murder Must Be Done

She died in his arms, and the tears ran unchecked down his cheeks.

His tall, dark, handsome frame shook with his sobs. She was too young and too lovely to die.

'Oh, my darling!' he cried brokenly. 'My darling! Without you, how will I go on living?'

And there was her face in close-up, serene and very beautiful in death — all glowing, like. And, up in the television control-room, the producer cried, 'Hold it! Hold it! Long fade!' and there were tears in his eyes, too.

Then — 'All right,' he sighed. 'Captions.'

And, as the credits started to climb the TV screens in ten — no, fifteen — million homes throughout Britain, there wasn't a dry eye in a single house.

'You were marvellous, Dorothea, darling! Just marvellous!' the producer told her, holding her hands in his own. And he was tall, dark, and handsome, too. 'Will you — I mean — would you — I mean — '

He stammered, tongue-tied by her beauty. She smiled a slow, serene smile. He wanted to ask her to marry him. They all did. She thought it was a bit of a bore, really.

Then the phone calls came flooding in, jamming the studio switchboard. The leading actor in the country was pleading with her again to star opposite him in one of his films. Another star was ringing up — begging . . .

She was Dorothea Winters, world-renowned star of stage, screen, and television.

She was also Doll Winters, machine operative, of Levinson Structural Steel Fabrications Limited, and the monotonous rhythmic clacking of her capstan had started her day-dreaming again.

She glanced quickly at the clock on the factory wall, glad it was almost time to knock off for the day. She switched off her lathe with the manageress's jackal eye on her, tossed her head to show she didn't care, and walked to the girls' cloakroom to clean up.

Other girls were there before her, chattering like magpies. Blondes, brunettes, and redheads of all assorted shapes and sizes. 'So I told him straight, I said, you're old enough to know better.' Someone sniggered. 'There was Mick and me in this caravan, see, and he said — '

Doll Winters listened absently as she washed cutting oil off her hands. She had heard it all before, and she didn't believe half of it. She didn't want to believe the other half. Doll read *Teenage Romances* and dreamt of pure, undying love. It seemed rather hard to find in this part of Tooting Bec.

She stripped off her coverall, hung it on a peg, and walked back past her machine as the buzzer rasped. She dived into the queue that was forming by the time clock, grabbed her card out of the rack and stamped it. Then she was outside, walking through the main gate of the small engineering factory where she worked. Drudgery from nine till five, then . . .

The pale sunlight laid a yellow film over blackened brick walls. A pimply-faced youth standing on a street corner, looked her over and whistled. 'How about a film tonight, luscious?'

Doll tossed her head. 'Get lost! Why don't you?' She moved on, tugging down the tail of her fluffy fawn sweater. Eighteen, petite, and curvaceous in all the right places, Doll moved with a wiggle that tantalized the callow male eye. Any male eye. Below the fluffy fawn sweater she wore a tight skirt and stilettoes.

'*Chérie* . . . ' purred the elegant Frenchman, bending to kiss her finger-tips, 'rarely 'ave I ze pleasure of meeting such grace, such beauty, such enchant-ment . . . '

'Why, dontcha look where you're going?' growled a fish-wife voice.

Doll Winters swerved round a bus queue which she saw only dimly, as if through a mist. She was lost in new fantasy.

' . . . Such bravery must be rewarded.

4

This young girl at the risk of her own life, dashed into the street to snatch up a small boy in front of a double-decker bus at the height of the rush hour. Such heroism . . . '

Doll Winters wiggled through Tooting's busy streets to the bed-sitter she rented not far from the Tube, wiggling back to a fish-and-chip tea with her landlady. She wished something exciting would happen. Something *really* exciting. She didn't care what.

And, though she didn't know it, something was going to happen. Though she didn't know it, her dream of excitement was about to turn into nightmare.

Though she didn't know it, she was wiggling her way towards a date with — murder.

★   ★   ★

The name Tooting may or may not be derived from 'Tot', signifying homestead; from the name of the Saxon chief, Tota; or from 'toot', meaning to peep out.

Historians are reluctant to commit themselves on this point.

But they all agree on the derivation of 'Bec'.

After the Norman conquest, the land hereabouts was handed over to monks from the Abbey of Bec, in Normandy. And, no doubt, it was a pleasant patch of English countryside then; remote, in those days, from London; just a few cottages surrounded by cornfields.

It has changed.

Today, Tooting Bec is a parish of Wandsworth, part of the gigantic suburban complex that sprawls south of the Thames. The old Roman road, Stane Street, passes this way to reach London from Chichester, and remains solidly jammed with vans, buses and cars during the rush hours.

For, besides being a dormitory for City workers, Tooting has its own industries. It is a noisy, busy and bustling place, and a thriving shopping centre in its own right. It has supermarkets and multiple stores, cinemas, record shops and espresso bars. And it has a multiplicity of hoardings, the art galleries of our affluent society: a free peepshow of beer and brassieres, corsets and cigarettes.

At night, the skyline is a fantasy of chimneys and television aerials illuminated by blazing neon signs. And, below, radiating from the shopping centre like the strands of a spider's web, stretch rank upon rank of interminably long streets under sodium lighting, in which small houses are tight-packed together, characterless, and dreary.

After their day's work in factories, offices, and shops, people scurry like swarms of ants for their cars or red buses that carry them home, and pass newsagents' filled with 'adult' magazines — whose covers uniformly display what at first sight appears to be the elephantine and odd in the feminine form. But it could be a new evolution.

And then they are home, some to be instantly pinned down like butterflies by the fascination of the goggle-box in the corner. Others fill up their Pool's coupons, or go for a drink at the local, or take a bus to the dogs.

But all try to escape in one way or another: escape the drab loneliness of existence in a London suburb. And no arctic waste or illimitable desert is lonelier than any suburb of any large city.

Tooting Bec is both a way of life and an attitude of mind. Its people work hard at getting something out of that life. They hardly care — if they know at all — that Thomas Hardy once lived here. And not even Doctor Johnson's visits to Mrs. Thrale can compete with the hectic love affairs of a Hollywood idol.

The people here remember the bombing, the fishing on the common, and last year's holiday. They work overtime to pay off another installment on a second-hand car; a washing machine; a holiday.

Above all, they dream. They dream of the big win on the Pools that would mean escape from the rat-race of earning a living, and from these teeming streets, and from all the racketing noise.

For all save a few, however, it remains only a dream — perhaps luckily. For the people of Tooting Bec are, in fact, hardened to their way of life and though they would never believe it and would laugh the suggestion to scorn, they'd certainly miss 'The Bec's' sights, smells, and sounds.

★   ★   ★

Murder was such an unpleasant word, Mr. Gerald Dodd thought through the low murmur of bassoons in Tchaikovsky's *Pathetique*.

Sad music suited both his mood and his long face.

Accident, Mr. Gerald Dodd decided, sounded much better than murder. And it would look better, too. An accident had been at the back of his mind for some time, and now circumstances were pushing it to the front.

Mr. Gerald Dodd was not a violent man by nature. He was reluctant to kill, but he was fast becoming quite desperate. He was being forced into killing by circumstances beyond his control.

He sat hunched in an armchair in the big living room of his semi-detached suburban villa in Norbury in South

London, only vaguely aware of the groaning brass blaring from the expensive radiogram, and well-nigh oblivious of his wife, Janet, and his son, Paul.

Paul, small and stocky, dark-haired and seven years of age, pored intently over a jigsaw puzzle of a farmyard littering the carpet. The boy's lips moved petulantly. 'Where's the bit with the horse's head?' he complained. 'I can't find the horse's head, Mum.'

'Shhh!' Janet whispered.

She was blonde, and pretty in a bold kind of way, but turning blowsy at twenty-eight. She darted a quick glance at her husband. She knew how Gerald hated to be disturbed when he was thinking. And she knew he was thinking now because he was frowning and tugging the lobe of an ear.

An accident . . . Gerald Dodd brooded, sitting there in the living room of his Norbury villa. An accident . . .

Mr. Gerald Dodd's villa was a nice house surrounded by other nice houses, all inhabited by very nice people. Or were they? Appearances, as in Gerald Dodd's case, could be deceptive. Mr. Gerald Dodd was a self-made crook, and proud of it — though he'd never contemplated murder before.

Now he was being compelled to contemplate it.

The room throbbed with sobbing strings and anxious horns. Damn it, Dodd thought, it was an inescapable fact: something just had to be done about Gillespie — and soon.

Gillespie was bleeding him white. Under the threat of exposure, Gillespie was putting the black on Gerald Dodd. Gillespie was a man who knew too much about Gerald Dodd's crooked activities. And Gillespie was threatening to sing — loud and clear — to the police unless he was paid, and paid regularly. For months, Dodd had had to buy his silence on the never-never plan.

Never be sure that Gillespie wouldn't blab to the police anyway. That was one thing. The man drank too much. And never be rid of Gillespie's inordinate demands for ever more and more money.

Silence is proverbially regarded as

golden. Gillespie's silence was fast becoming as expensive as nothing less than pure platinum. Gillespie was making the mistake of most blackmailers: being too greedy, driving his victim too far . . . And this was why Gerald Dodd had been forced to the point of planning cold-blooded murder.

He made up his mind. Now. Tonight. He looked at the clock over the mantelpiece. There was time. He'd had the murder plan in his mind for a while past, every detail of it. It only needed to be carried through.

He rose and switched off the radiogram. The *Pathetique* stopped in the middle of a brilliant coda. Dodd said in a tight voice 'Got to go out, Janet. Got to see a man.'

'Yes, Gerald,' she agreed, not quite looking at him.

Dodd wondered: how much did she guess? They'd been married for ten years. She must suspect something. Then he smiled faintly. It was unlikely she was thinking of murder . . .

He padded into the hall and looked at

himself in the mirror. He looked his forty years, with his thinning hair and down-turned mouth, and the paunch starting under his shiny serge suit. He ran a hand over his unshaven jawbone.

There was no point in shaving, nor in putting on a collar and tie. He wrapped a dark scarf round his throat. Anything else? He felt irritated with himself for being so vague. He couldn't afford to be vague about committing a murder . . .

Gloves . . .

He picked up an old pair and jammed his bowler hat down over his head.

Outside the house, he hesitated about taking his car, a Rover Saloon, and decided to walk. It was not more than a hundred yards to his garage on the London Road. His stomach began to rumble, and he winced. Damn it, he'd told Janet often enough to make sure that his steak was well done. He popped an indigestion tablet into his mouth.

The garage sprawled over a corner lot under a big sign bearing his name: G. DODD — CAR MART. A front for his real business.

Seven out of ten of the cars he dealt in were 'hot' — though the police didn't know it. He had always been careful. He had watched his p's and q's over the years. He had built up a good business. It had brought him everything that he needed.

But everything was now in jeopardy. Gillespie was driving him into the ground.

And so Mr. Gerald Dodd was being forced to the point of committing the ultimate crime of murder.

2

Not According To Plan

Gillespie swayed on long, lanky legs. His raincoat was frayed and dirty. His thin face was flushed, and his breath reeked of stale beer. A limp cigarette dangled under his bulbous, blue-veined nose.

And he was boasting again. What an overbearing loudmouth he was!

'As easy as taking candy from a kid,' he was saying. 'Just picked it up outside the Festival Hall. Be hours before the owner gets out. Time for a quick paint job, and — '

Loathing the man, Gerald Dodd forced himself to listen.

Gillespie was helping him. Gillespie's fingerprints would be everywhere on the blue Mini that he'd just brought in. The car he had just stolen.

Mouth twisted down, Gerald Dodd thought: Isn't this Gillespie all over? He's bleeding me white, but he still can't keep his hands from fiddling and thieving. He's getting a fortune from me every week — but still he steals cars . . .

The two men were in the spray shop at the back of the garage, where two other stolen cars, which had recently been given 'the treatment' were being fitted out with new number plates.

The blue Mini looked fine, except for a scratch along one side panel where Gillespie had grazed something.

'Listen, Gerry — ' Gillespie said thickly. And Dodd hated being called Gerry by anyone, and particularly by a creature like Gillespie. 'Listen, Gerry — ' and inwardly Dodd squirmed.

But he had to put up with it — for the moment. Gillespie had the whip hand. 'Listen, Gerry,' Gillespie said. 'I need some dough quick. Lotsa dough. What about five hundred tonight?' He leered. 'Not on the car. I'm not asking for that. No — you know — on account of our little arrangement . . . '

The bite again.

Still leering, Gillespie went on: 'Then

you can pay me for the car at the end of the week.'

Gerald Dodd faced him, hatred as flat and sour as bile in his stomach. But he reached a swift decision, and he kept his voice level. This was fine. It fitted in with his plans perfectly. 'Okay,' he said.

Gillespie clapped him on the shoulder, and again Dodd squirmed inwardly. 'Good old Gerry!' Gillespie said. 'Yeah! Somehow I knew I could rely on you.'

He was grinning all over his face.

It was only with an effort that Dodd kept his seething hatred out of his voice. 'You couldn't have brought that car in at a better time,' he said. 'I can do with it. Fill her up, will you?'

And, abruptly, he turned away and stepped into his office. There his foreman, Don Westerly, joined him.

Westerly was a stocky figure in mechanic's oily overalls. He had odd-coloured eyes, one blue and one brown, and these gave him a sinister appearance. He closed the door of the office and leaned against it looking hard at Gerald Dodd.

'That Gillespie's dangerous,' he said flatly. 'You got to take care of him, boss, or we'll all end up inside. You got to!'

How little you know, Dodd thought. 'I am,' he said. 'I'm going to do it tonight.'

Don Westerly looked very relieved. 'Thought you were going soft,' he growled. 'Gillespie should have been taken care of long before this. He talks too much, especially when he's tanked up. And that is a fact.'

The foreman watched Gerald Dodd jerk open a drawer. 'You want any help?'

Gerald Dodd shook his head. 'Not me, Don. When there's dirty work to do, I do it myself. That's always been my motto. No slip-ups that way . . . '

He took a spanner from the drawer and hefted it in his hand

It was a large, double-ended spanner, ancient and scarred from long years of use. He wiped it carefully with an oily rag and slipped it into his pocket.

Then he found a street-map; spread it out; studied it. He checked the time. 'In just under two hours, Don, Gillespie won't worry us any more.'

'That's what I like to hear, boss.'

Dodd went back to the Mini. 'Get in, Gillespie,' he said. 'You're driving.'

Gillespie tossed down his cigarette butt. 'Look here, Gerry,' he protested. 'I was just thinking of picking up my dough and — '

Dodd said flatly, 'If you're going to have your money tonight, I've got to see a man. Now come on.'

'I'm feelin' dry — '

'Later,' Dodd promised.

A little unwillingly, Gillespie slid into the driving seat of the Mini and started the engine. 'Take it steady, and for Pete's sake don't hit anything,' Dodd said, glancing down at the gloves he was wearing. He must remember not to take them off.

'Where to, Gerry?'

'Tooting High Street — I'll direct you when we get there . . . '

Gillespie used side streets between rows of grey houses where the street lamps were few and sporadic. Dodd stopped him once and went into an off-licence and returned with a bottle of

19

whisky. 'We might have to wait for this fellow I've got to see,' he explained.

Gillespie drove on with new interest. They reached the High Street and Dodd gave further directions. Gillespie manoeuvred the Mini precisely. They settled down to wait, engine switched off and lights out, parked at the top of a steep incline leading down to the main road.

Dodd had picked out this spot some time before.

There was a broken-down fence on his near side affording a gap through which he could observe oncoming traffic. A huge elm tree grew in the garden of an empty house, throwing dark shadow. The only light was the reflection from cars passing in and out of London. He was parked ten yards up from the main thoroughfare.

It was not a busy road at night, but the traffic was fast-moving, and sometimes the lorries were heavily loaded. He'd checked on one. It made regular time every night, coming fast. It always traveled too fast to be able to stop in a hurry.

He handed Gillespie the whisky bottle. 'Help yourself,' he said generously.

Gillespie took a long swig and wiped the neck of the bottle, but he did not offer it back. 'Who are we waiting for, Gerry?' he asked.

'Just a man,' Dodd answered. 'A certain man. And he'll be coming in a certain lorry.'

He watched the road for its telltale lights; two bright arcs low down, and a single orange lamp high on the left side. He listened for the sound of its engine. He knew that, too.

Gillespie poured more whisky down his throat, and Dodd remembered the past. Before he'd even left school he'd decided that dishonesty was the best policy: that crime did pay. He'd started with petty pilfering. In his teens it had been car-stealing. Then he'd taken to dealing in stolen cars, and now he had a prosperous business and a respectable home and he wasn't going to let Gillespie spoil everything.

He glanced at his watch. Almost time. He felt for the heavy spanner in his pocket. Then, briefly, he tried to analyze his emotions.

He was going to kill a man, and yet he felt nothing. He wasn't sweating, cold, or impatient. Come what may, the man sitting next to him had got to be eliminated. He worried a little, for he ought to feel *something*. He checked again. Yes . . . there was anxiety . . . but only in case the lorry did not turn up on time.

Gillespie was the vilest kind of blackmailer, that was what it boiled down to. Gillespie represented an inevitable ruination of everything he had built up over the years.

Gillespie didn't work at the garage, and Dodd didn't know anyone who would miss him. To everyone else at the garage, Gillespie was just a man who brought cars in — and who talked too damned much in his cups.

Again Dodd looked at his watch. Five minutes to wait. He turned his head sideways, studying Gillespie. The whisky had got him . . . he was fumbling, trying to light a cigarette.

Gerald Dodd covertly brought the

spanner out of his pocket, and gripped it tightly in his gloved hand.

Then he saw the lights he had been waiting for: two arcs, one orange. *Now!* He flung open the car door; twisted inwards; flung up the spanner to strike.

Gillespie's head came around fast and, for one brief moment, the drink-sodden eyes registered fear.

Then the spanner smashed down with tremendous force, and his skull cracked like an eggshell.

Dodd was out of the car now and watching the heavy lorry speeding along the main road at the foot of the incline, timing it. At exactly the right moment, he jerked off the handbrake and slammed the door on the Mini. The car began to roll down the incline, gathering speed as it went. It plunged directly into the path of the onrushing lorry.

And that was when the girl screamed.

★　★　★

Doll Winters had left the Plaza cinema in a dream.

She had seen an American gangster film, and now she was a gun-moll.

'Over my dead body,' she gritted, finger crooked round the trigger of her pearl-handled automatic. 'You'll never take him from me . . . '

A pool of light spilled across the pavement as the last house crowd poured out through the cinema's foyer and side exits. A queue formed at the bus stop across the road. Doll Winters walked on.

A leather-jacketed youth with brilliantined hair and chisel-toed Italian shoes leaned against a shop window filled with surgical appliances. He looked Doll up and down, and jingled the coins in his pocket. He admired her slim figure and long shapely legs, and offered. 'See you home, baby?'

Doll looked straight through him. She sniffed. 'Drop dead!' And she wriggled on along the High Street all alone. All the boys around here were the same, she thought. They had the same crude approach, and the same objective. Ugh! No finesse.

She had a long walk ahead of her, but

she didn't mind that. After all, she had her dream. Reality faded . . . she'd avenge her dead lover, for sure. She'd get that G-man if it was the last thing she did . . .

Later, vaguely aware that darkness had closed in around her, she paused. She stopped a little way along a side road. Where was she now? She peered uncertainly at a huge elm tree, blank empty windows, a straggling wooden fence. Then she recognized the hairdresser's across the road, and she brightened. She was all right. The second turning, and —

That was the moment she saw the parked Mini. It stood, dark and motionless, on an incline. It was pointed at the main road.

A thrill ran through her.

There had been a parked car in the film. She saw the glow of a cigarette from the driver's seat.

. . . The G-man took a long drag at his butt and jerked a gun from his pocket . . .

Doll's eyes widened as the offside car door suddenly jerked open. A man swiftly twisted himself out of the car. She saw a hand raised; a glint of metal. She saw the metal streak down; heard a sickening thud. The next instant, the car was rolling down towards the main road.

Doll stared — breathless — fascinated — not quite able to separate fantasy from reality, her clenched knuckles hard against her teeth.

She glimpsed a speeding lorry piled high with empty crates. She saw the Mini plunging down the incline towards inevitable collision. She heard the scream of brakes as the lorry driver tried to swerve, and the ear-splitting, tearing crash that testified that he'd failed.

Then Doll knew she was witnessing a real-life drama. Then she screamed.

And the man who had scrambled out of the Mini before it had started off on its suicidal lunging plunge down the incline into the main road wheeled to face her. For a second that seemed to stretch taut to eternity, they stared at each other.

The man wore a bowler hat, and held a, spanner. A big, heavy spanner.

Then he came for her.

Doll turned and ran, and he ran after her. She ran hard. She was young, and she was frightened; he was middle-aged, and out of condition. She heard him panting along behind as she tore through the dark, empty streets, terror riding her. His footsteps fell further and further behind.

Nevertheless, she didn't stop running until she had reached the front door of her lodgings, fumbled the key into the lock, and slammed the door after her.

She sagged back against the wall, gasping; trembling.

She had seen the man's face.

'That you, Doll?' her landlady called. 'Doll, that you — ?'

Doll Winters expelled a long, tremulous breath. 'Yes, Miss Legge — ' she got out ' — yes, it's me.'

★ ★ ★

Mr. Gerald Dodd ran as fast as his short legs and bulging waistline would allow. He cursed himself for not having had a car waiting, but he hadn't wanted a witness . . . and now he had one.

He sweated as he chased the girl. He'd

27

been too intent on watching the lorry and timing 'the accident' to notice her standing there, watching his every move. Damn it, she must have seen everything! This slim, pretty chit of a girl could land him with a murder charge! He had to catch her, and stop her mouth.

He ran hard, legs aching from the unaccustomed exercise, gulping air into his tortured lungs. The girl was moving fast. She was getting away. He remembered her face, a pale moon of horror, accentuating the redness of her parted lips and the green of her eye shadow. She was young; a sexy piece, he thought irrelevantly.

Now all he saw of her was a rear view of a tight red skirt and flashing stiletto heels as she vanished round a corner. When he himself turned the corner she was already out of sight. He slackened speed and went on half-heartedly. Which way had she gone? He wandered in a circle, through dreary suburban streets without finding her.

Mr. Gerald Dodd swore. So now his carefully planned accident was labelled murder. And his stomach was acting up again. He placed an indigestion tablet on his tongue, and sucked noisily. What the hell was he going to do?

He tugged at the lobe of his ear. What would she do? That was the sixty-four thousand dollar question. If she went to the police . . . he shuddered, remembering Janet and his comfortable home.

He *had* to find her.

Then he discovered that he was still holding the spanner, sticky with blood, and he tossed it among some junk behind a hedge at the bottom of a neglected garden. Hell, he could do with a large Scotch, and all the damned pubs were shut.

He dug coins out of his pocket, and found a call box. He phoned the garage.

'Don — ?' he said. 'Don — it's gone wrong!'

3

Doll In Danger

Miss Doll Winters rose late, after a restless night. She returned from the bathroom and pulled her fluffy fawn sweater over her head. She wasn't going to the factory this morning. She had her duty to do.

She dreamed a while about doing her duty. She was the sole witness to murder. . . . She was in the witness box at the Old Bailey. 'And this is the man you saw on the night in question?' Counsel for the Prosecution pointed a lean finger. Her answer rang out loud and clear. 'Yes. That is the man!'

Miss Legge's voice was even louder. 'You want any breakfast, Doll?'

She went downstairs to the kitchen and she ate bacon and fried bread with a dreamy expression. Her landlady, Miss Legge, looked at her — suspiciously.

'You in trouble, gel?'

Doll ignored this insinuation on her good character. She left the house and wiggled her way towards the police station, pausing to look up at the blue lamp before she went inside.

It was her first time ever inside a police station, and the bare, barrack-like atmosphere had its effect upon her. Her eyes clouded over. Unbidden, another daydream began to take shape in her mind . . .

Then somebody coughed.

It was the duty sergeant. He had a face like raw beef. He was looking inquiringly at Doll from behind his desk. He said: 'Yes, miss? Can I help you?'

Doll Winters recollected her duty, and looked about her. There was a young constable whom she knew vaguely. 'Yes,' she said brightly. 'I've come about the murder.'

'Murder, miss?' The sergeant looked grave. The young constable put a hand over his mouth. He'd been on this beat long enough to know Doll Winters and her daydreams. Everyone knew Doll.

'Yes, last night,' she said. 'I saw it all. There was this man in a bowler hat with a spanner. He hit him and the car went under a lorry. The man in the bowler hat had a sad face and he chased me all the way home. Well . . . not quite all the way . . . I escaped.'

The young constable said casually. 'Good film, Doll?'

'Smashing! All about a young girl who got caught up with a mob and . . . ' Her voice died away. The young constable and the sergeant had exchanged glances. And the young constable's glance was easily interpreted. It said, 'See, sarge . . . ? See . . . ?'

Doll Winters said: 'You don't believe me, do you?'

The sergeant turned the pages of a ledger. He spoke heavily. 'I have here,' he said, 'a report of an accident involving a lorry . . . and a blue Mini. The Mini had been stolen from outside the Festival Hall. The man driving it when it smashed into the lorry was drunk. He was killed outright in the crash. The time of the accident was ten-fifty last night . . . '

He looked steadily at Doll.

He said, 'If you were a witness to this accident, young lady, I want you to tell me exactly what you saw.'

'I was a witness . . . but it wasn't an accident,' Doll Winters insisted. 'He hit him with a spanner. The man in the bowler hat did.'

The police sergeant and the young constable eyed each other again. And then the police sergeant sighed. 'We'd best take a statement.'

The young constable wrote down all that Doll Winters said, and then read the statement back, and she signed it. But she knew that they didn't believe her. Well, they'd find out! Then she'd be really important. The star witness. Doll enjoyed a good courtroom drama . . .

'Nothing else, miss?' the sergeant said. 'Your description of the murderer is a bit vague.'

Doll racked her brains. 'It was dark . . . and I didn't stop to ask his name.'

'Of course, miss. It was dark.' The sergeant closed the ledger with a heavy hand. 'Please,' he said earnestly, 'don't go repeating any of this outside.'

Doll sniffed. Coppers were all the same. Doubting Thomases. She didn't know why she had bothered with them. As she went out, she heard the sound of soft laughter.

Across the street, a man with odd-coloured eyes folded his racing paper and followed her.

★ ★ ★

After lunch — beans-on-toast in a café — Doll went to the factory as usual, but she couldn't seem to do anything right. She had things on her mind. She was glad when the buzzer sounded and she could breathe fresh air again. But out on the street she had the feeling that someone was following.

She hopped on a bus.

'Not going out, Doll?' Miss Legge asked after tea.

'Not tonight. I didn't get much sleep last night — think I'll turn in early.'

She ran a bath and soaked for half an hour, thinking about the man in the bowler hat. The memory of him made her uneasy. She was sure now that someone had followed her home and was watching the house. She was equally sure that whoever it was who had followed her had no connection at all with the police.

The police hadn't believed her story, but she knew she'd seen murder done. And the murderer knew that she knew.

Doll had seen too many gangster films not to realize what that implied . . . 'You ain't gonna do no talkin', baby! We're gonna shut yo' mouth permanent!'

Suddenly the bath water held a chill. Doll got out and towelled herself dry, slipped into her dressing gown and returned to her room. The miniature bolt on her bedroom door gave her no great feeling of security, so she pushed the old-fashioned washstand across the doorway. Its rickety legs shuddered and squealed over the oilcloth.

'What you doing, Doll?' her landlady called out.

'Oh . . . nothing, Miss Legge.'

Doll surveyed the barricade with little satisfaction. A rickety washstand, a rose-coloured basin and a jug of water weren't going to keep a killer at bay.

She was very uneasy.

She turned her picture of the latest pop idol to the wall while she slipped out of her dressing gown and wriggled into baby doll pyjamas. Then she switched off the light, crossed to the window, pulled back an edge of curtain and peered out.

Was that a man standing across the street, or just a shadow . . . She couldn't be sure.

More uneasy than ever, Doll Winters quickly climbed into bed and pulled the blankets up over her head.

★　★　★

Westerly said, 'I followed her like you told me, boss. The coppers didn't seem to take very much notice. The girl works at the Stafford Engineering place . . . that's her room, with the light on, first floor front.'

As Gerald Dodd looked up, the light went out. He regarded the darkened window mournfully. She was only a kid, after all. It was a pity she had to die. But if the police ever did get around to investigating her story, they might think that there was something in it. And she was the only person who could identify him as Gillespie's killer.

'Right, Don,' he said. 'You lose yourself. This is my job.'

'Okay, boss.' Westerly glanced at Dodd, wondering about him. Did he have the nerve to go through with it? He'd better have! If he was picked up, Westerly stood to lose a good job and an easy six hundred pounds a week. More than that, he'd cop a prison sentence. 'I'll be in the car round the corner when you're through,' he said. He walked away.

Gerald Dodd looked at the house across the street: an old semi-detached, with ivy covering the dirty red bricks. The ground floor had bay windows of the sash type, so there would be no difficulty about getting in.

He looked down at his gloved hands, and curled the fingers tentatively. The girl would be sleeping, he thought. It would be easy enough . . .

Then he realized that he was sweating.

He'd been able to kid himself that Gillespie's death had really been an accident. But not this time. Not when he planned to strangle an innocent young girl in cold blood. He eased up the rim of his bowler and settled it again on his head.

He waited.

The street was deserted, and presently the street-lamps went out. In the darkness, he crossed to the opposite pavement, his footsteps echoing hollowly.

There was no gate.

He moved up three feet of concrete path and stepped into long grass below a bay window. He opened his pocketknife and forced the ancient catch with the blade. The window creaked as he raised it. The tiny sound grated on his nerves in the stillness.

He moved a flowerpot just inside the window, and climbed through. The front room was dusty, the furniture covered with sheets. Victorian bric-a-brac lined the mantelpiece.

Gerald Dodd eased open the door of the room and crossed the narrow hallway beyond. He paused in the darkness at the bottom of the stairs, listening. He went up cautiously, fingers screening the light from his torch.

A worn carpet muffled his footsteps, but his breathing sounded like a grampus snorting. He tried to control it. He reached the upper landing. There were two doors: one back and one front. He padded towards the door at the front, facing the street, and placed an ear against the wooden panelling.

A faint sound of regular breathing reached him.

The girl was asleep, all right.

He gripped the doorknob, turned it, and pushed gently. The door didn't budge. He frowned. The door must be bolted on the inside, he guessed. But that wasn't going to stop him.

The bolt would only be a cheap thing from Woolworth's. One good shove would force the staple. Of course, it couldn't be done silently. But he'd simply have to crash into the room, kill, and get out again as quickly as possible. Speed would replace silence in ensuring his safety. Yes, it was as simple as that.

He tensed himself; got his shoulder down. For a split second, he was utterly immobile. Then he hurled himself forward.

He hit the door hard with his shoulder, and the bolt gave. The door rocketed inwards in an explosion of sound, and he followed it in.

But, the next moment, he tripped. He nearly pitched forward headlong. Furniture splintered and crashed down in front of him. Something struck him a numbing blow on the arm and threw water all over him. For an instant, Gerald Dodd was dazed.

And, in that instant, the girl woke up — screaming. And a light went on in the back room. A woman's voice called out: 'Doll . . . ?'

Gerald Dodd panicked.

The girl he needed to kill was yelling her head off, and he was still nowhere near her. And the other woman — the one in the back room behind him — sounded as if she was getting out of bed at the double.

Gerald Dodd ran.

He lunged for the stairs, and he plunged down them four treads at a time. He was sweating as he scrambled out through the ground floor window through which he'd entered the house. He sprinted away

And as he ran, huffing and puffing, so he savagely cursed. He'd muffed his chance . . . beaten by a mere slip of a girl! He groaned aloud, regretting he'd ever got himself involved in the gentle art of murder.

He was going to have even more cause to regret it in the days that followed.

4

Calling Mr. Brand

'I'm not stopping here to be murdered,' Doll Winters said, over breakfast. She was dressed and packed — baby-doll pyjamas, pop idol pin-up, and *Teenage Romances* all in her case. She was ready to leave.

'Really, Doll,' Miss Legge chided. She was a bright little bird of a woman in her late sixties, with old-fashioned ultra-feminine clothes and an improbable mane of henna-red hair.

She pecked at her food; she pecked at conversation. She pecked at her lodger — Doll Winters — but this always kindly. She said: 'You and your imagination, child! Very likely, your visitor last night was only an over-ardent admirer.' She paused. 'Where will you go?'

'I dunno,' Doll said. 'No good going to the police again. Maybe I'll go back home.'

But she spoke without any show of enthusiasm.

She had just over three hundred pounds in a Post Office savings account, and no really close friends. Who would shelter her from a cold-blooded killer? Like the heroine of the film, she would have to take it on the lam . . .

. . . It was a squalid waterfront dive. But with the cops hard on her trail since the breakout, and Bugsy Malone looking for her to close her trap permanent, she couldn't be choosy. 'How much, Ma . . . ?'

Reality impinged through the world of dreams. 'Your tea's getting cold, Doll.'

Doll Winters gulped down the almost cold cup of tea, and then rose. She hadn't slept at all after her midnight visitation. She had just sat there waiting for the killer to come back. She knew he'd have to try again. He couldn't afford to let her talk.

She opened the front door and looked out at the empty street, then walked hurriedly away from the house. She was wearing a scarlet swagger coat and carrying a small suitcase, and she hadn't got any good idea of where she was going. Just away. Somewhere safe — if she could find such a place.

She dreamed a little . . . and found herself in the street where she'd been born. A row of small terraced houses, with a smell of tight-shut windows and stuffy belongings that were never aired. What sort of a reception would she get, she wondered. She knocked on the drably brown door.

Her mother opened the door and immediately sniffed. 'Oh, It's you! And what do you want, Doll?' Her voice was shrill and unpleasant. She stood with arms akimbo, an ogress guarding the castle entrance. 'You left of your own accord, me gal, so if you're in trouble don't bring it here. I told you you're no good — so stay outa my hair.'

'I need a place to hide for a few days,' Doll said patiently. I — '

'Hide, is it?' Mrs. Winters hawked in her throat. 'Don't you go bringing no coppers round here!' And she slammed the door in her daughter's face.

Doll turned away.

After that she walked aimlessly. She thought it would have been different if her Dad had lived, but her Mum . . . she shook her head. Her Mum had never wanted her, and that was the truth of it.

But she had to find a roof somewhere, and it wasn't going to be easy. Since she'd left home, she'd had a variety of jobs, always moving on, never taking a steady boy or making firm friends. The police didn't believe her murder story, and her mother didn't want her. She was all alone . . .

She bought an early edition of the *Evening Post* to check the Rooms Vacant column, but found her interest caught and held by a photograph on the front page. It was a portrait of a man with expressive eyes and mobile lips. He was middle-aged by Doll's standards, but all the same there was something immensely reassuring about him. He looked like a man who wouldn't stand any nonsense.

There was a story under the picture. Doll read it avidly. It seemed the man pictured on the front page was called

Brand, and he was a detective — a private eye. Suddenly, Doll knew that this was the man for her. He wouldn't stand around and let her be foully murdered, like the cops. He'd round up the gang in no time flat and then . . .

Doll Winters sighed romantically.

She read the newspaper story again, this time more closely. It appeared that Simon Brand was already famous. He'd solved murders that had baffled the police. And he had offices in Berkeley Square.

Well, Doll Winters thought as she began to move purposefully in the direction of the nearest Underground station, as of now Mr. Brand had got himself a new client.

★ ★ ★

Back in his comfortable semi-detached house in Norbury, Gerald Dodd's long face was white and haggard.

There was a plaster on his cheek where he'd nicked himself shaving. He looked the picture of a worried man as he gnawed at his fingernails.

The panic within him had subsided to some extent, but he was still badly scared — and it was with a feeling of desperation that he waited for the telephone to ring.

His wife, Janet, was busy in their 'luxury' kitchen, and Paul had already left for school.

Dodd looked round his comfortable home with the air of a man seeing it for the last time. When the phone rang he nearly jumped out of his skin. 'Yes? Who is it?'

A gruff voice answered. 'Westerly here, boss. The girl's on the run. Packed a case and left. I'll stick with her till she settles, then ring you again.'

Dodd sweated. 'Yes, yes. Let me know. For Pete's sake don't lose her . . . ' He shuddered as a memory flooded through him. The memory of the girl standing only feet away from the Mini and watching him smash Gillespie's head in with a spanner. She had to be eliminated fast.

'Yes, let me know where she settles. Then I'll take care of it.'

'Will do, boss,' Westerly said, and the line went dead.

Dodd wiped his face with a clean handkerchief. He needed a drink, and he needed one badly. He walked into the kitchen, jerked open the door of the refrigerator, and took out a bottle of strong beer. He banged the cap off against the edge of the kitchen table, put the neck of the bottle to his mouth and drank in great gulps.

Janet watched him, silent for a moment, then she said gently, 'It's a bit early for that, isn't it?'

Dodd glared at her. He'd forgotten her, forgotten where he was, forgotten everything except his need to drown out what he must do. He must silence the girl. She was the only witness to the murder and, once she was taken care of, he could stop worrying and relax again.

'What is it?' his wife asked.

'Nothing, Janet — it's nothing!'

She twisted a loose button on her housecoat. She had let herself go steadily downhill over the last few years, and she knew it. She had let herself go ever since the birth of Paul, in fact.

She hadn't wanted another child. That was the truth of the matter.

And so, without thinking about it, she'd just let herself go: subconsciously making herself less and less attractive to this man Gerald Dodd, her husband.

It had been an unthinking defence against his ardour, and it had cooled it all right. He didn't bother her very much now.

Maybe that was the trouble . . .

She said, 'Something's worrying you, Gerald. You've got something on your mind. Well — ' her mouth trembled, ' — you might just as well tell me now as let me find out for myself later. There's Paul to think of — '

'Shut it!' Dodd snapped. What did she suspect? What went on under that somewhat frowsy blonde hair? 'Just stay out of it!' he growled. 'It's better for you to know nothing.'

Janet Dodd sighed. Tears had welled up in her eyes. 'I know,' she said. 'It's another woman. I should never have let myself go like this . . . you're tired of me . . . '

And abruptly she swung away.

She ran out of the kitchen, and he heard her crying. Dodd was startled. What the hell . . . ? You never knew what went on in a woman's head!

Then he forgot about her.

He had enough on his mind already without worrying over a jealous woman. He had to accomplish Doll Winter's death in double quick time, or else he was deep in real, dangerous trouble.

★   ★   ★

Detective-Sergeant Heighway was also a worried man. He sat alone in the CID room on the first floor of Tooting police station, studying reports. The driver of the crashed Mini had been identified: Sean Gillespie, a small-time crook and car-thief.

Sergeant Heighway rubbed a nicotine-stained finger across his slim moustache. There had been far too many car-thefts in the South London area of late. It was beginning to look as if they might be organized. All stations had been ordered to maintain a special watch.

Heighway carefully read through the doctor's report. Gillespie had been killed by a blow on the top of his skull. The body had been badly crushed under the impact of the collision but, by chance, the head had been left virtually unharmed. It was just one of those things.

Detective-Sergeant Heighway lit a cigarette, inhaled, and blew twin jets of smoke through his nostrils. Of course Gillespie could have cracked his skull when the lorry hit the Mini . . . the man must have been hurled about, but the explanation didn't quite satisfy him.

He turned back to the statement made by the girl, Winters. He read:

' . . . He hit him with a spanner before the car went under the lorry . . . '

Heighway kept this in mind as he re-read a section of the doctor's report. A large quantity of alcohol had been found in the deceased's stomach. Would a thief get drunk in possession of a stolen car?

There was something odd about the whole business, Heighway decided. Suspicion burgeoned in his mind.

Suppose it was murder . . . ? He sat stiffly in his hard-backed chair, forcing himself to face the issue squarely. He'd have to talk to the lorry driver, and to the girl, Winters. He had her address on the report sheet.

She'd be at work now, he thought. He'd have to find out where that was, and interview her. She had to be found. If she was telling the truth, and she'd seen murder done, she could be in very real danger. She'd have to be given protection.

He rose and reached for his hat, glancing at the address again. He'd have a word with the girl's landlady first . . .

But, by then, it was already too late. Doll Winters's landlady didn't know where she'd gone — only that it wasn't to work.

Doll Winters was, in fact, crossing London at that very moment. And she wasn't alone.

Never far away from her, unseen and unnoticed in London's omnipresent, hustling and bustling throng, there stalked a man with odd-coloured eyes.

Indefatigably, he tailed her — as relentless as Death.

★　★　★

The sun had been shining when Doll Winters had entered Tooting Broadway Tube station. But now, when she surfaced again at Green Park, the sky was grey and overcast.

A newspaper-seller in Piccadilly directed her along Berkeley Street just as it started to rain — and rain heavily. All around Berkeley Square, when Doll Winters reached it, water drummed down on large, highly-polished Rolls-Royces and other expensive cars, all parked almost bumper-to-bumper alongside the kerb.

Doll paused in the rain to look up at an imposing office block and, behind her, the odd-coloured eyes of the man called Westerly, Gerald Dodd's foreman, narrowed abruptly. What was she up to now?

But Doll wasn't up to anything, exactly. She was just pausing, and looking, and thinking. Posh, she thought, eyeing the office block, and she had a momentary qualm. Perhaps that detective would expect a big fee.

. . . She looked at him through slitted, silky lids. Her voice was husky, and alluring. 'I can't pay you in money, Mr. Brand,' she murmured, 'But . . . '

She started to move again, determinedly. And now Westerly saw where she was heading, and swore violently under his breath. For a second it even looked as though he might try to intercept her. But she was moving too quickly for him and, glowering, he dropped back again. He saw her push through plate-glass swing doors and climb a short flight of stairs. She passed out of sight. Outside, on the pavement, Westerly pulled up his coat collar against the rain, and settled down to wait. And, inside —

Inside the building, at the head of the stairs, there was a door lettered in red: SIMON BRAND INVESTIGATIONS. Doll knocked, and opened the door.

A pretty brunette receptionist sat at a switchboard. She wasn't much older than Doll herself. 'Hello,' she said in a slightly breathless, but friendly voice. 'Can I help you?'

Doll waved her copy of the *Evening Post*. 'I want to see Mr. Brand. I saw murder done, and the killer's out to get me!'

The brunette looked somewhat startled. 'Mr. Brand is out of town on a case,' she said. 'Why don't you try the police?'

Doll laughed bitterly. 'I been to the cops. They don't believe me . . . they think I made it all up . . . so far as they are concerned, I can get bumped off and good riddance.'

She put down her suitcase, sat down, and crossed her slim, shapely legs. 'I'll wait,' she said decisively. 'When will Mr. Brand be getting back?'

The pretty brunette at the reception desk considered this question, but did not answer it. Instead, she said, 'Perhaps Mr. Brand's secretary can see you.' She rose and went quickly into another room.

Doll didn't mind waiting. At least she was safe here . . .

A tall, willowy honey-blonde came back with the brunette receptionist. Doll's earlier dream struck a submerged rock and foundered without a trace. Mr. Brand's secretary looked as if she had just stepped off the cover of a glossy magazine, and Doll knew she didn't stand a chance against this kind of competition. It wasn't fair!

'I'm going to wait here until I see Mr. Brand,' she announced firmly.

The blonde smiled. 'Suppose you come into my office and tell me all about it? Perhaps I can help you. My name is Miss Dean.'

Doll was reluctant. It was Mr. Brand she had come here to see . . . but she didn't want to be murdered, and she was badly scared. 'All right,' she agreed ungraciously. 'If you think it will do any good.'

'I'm sure it will.'

Doll sat in a comfortable armchair, and the blonde Miss Dean went behind a broad desk. 'You won't mind if I switch on the tape. Then Mr. Brand and Mr. Chandler can hear all you've got to tell me when they get back. It may be a day or two, I'm afraid. Cigarette?'

'I don't smoke,' Doll said promptly. 'But I'd like a choc-ice.'

Brand's secretary lifted a telephone. 'Marilyn? Will you pop out and get a choc-ice somewhere . . . ? Yes, I know it's raining!'

She pushed down a switch. 'Marla Dean recording. Now, Miss — er — '

'Doll Winters. From Tooting Bec. It was like this . . . '

And Doll told her story again.

Marla Dean listened without interrupting. When Doll had finished, she said, 'You didn't go back to the police then, after this man had tried to break into your room?'

'No — what was the use? Them coppers didn't believe nothing. Even my landlady thought it was some boy I'd given too much encouragement to . . . '

Marla made a note on her pad. The girl's landlady could check that part of her story. She wished Brand were there. This Miss Winters was obviously highly imaginative . . . but suppose her story were true? This girl had come to the offices of Simon Brand Investigations expecting help. If Marla turned her away and the killer got her, she could imagine what Brand would say. And rightly. Furthermore, she'd find it difficult to live with herself.

She made up her mind, and smiled confidently.

'All right, Miss Winters. I think it will be best if I keep you under cover until Mr. Brand returns. Then he will decide what to do. For tonight, you can sleep at my flat. That will be safe enough . . . '

But, for once, Simon Brand's capable secretary could not have been more wrong.

5

On The Run

Only once in the whole of his life had he known waiting as bad as this, Gerald Dodd thought.

That had been when his son Paul had been born. The baby had been overdue, and Janet had had to be induced.

Particularly he remembered the waiting at the hospital . . . as he waited now, deep in an armchair in Norbury, waited for the phone to ring.

The house was quiet with Janet out shopping. So quiet that the clock on the mantelpiece sounded like a homemade time bomb. Why didn't Westerly ring through? Where had the girl got to? He stared gloomily through the rain-washed windows, watching the water stream from his Rover Saloon parked outside by the kerb. He felt on edge, restless, and very frightened.

For all he knew, the police might be checking on the girl's story right at this very moment. If she ever got into a witness box . . . damn Gillespie to hell! If that lush had kept his mouth shut he wouldn't be in this mess!

The phone shrilled. He got a grip on his nerves. No more panic, he told himself. What had to be done must be done calmly. He lifted the receiver and said, 'Gerald Dodd speaking,' in something like his normal tone of voice.

'Westerly here, boss.' The garage foreman sounded nervous. 'The girl's finally settled somewhere, and you ain't going to like it when I tell you just where that is.'

Gerald Dodd's heart skipped a beat. 'The police?'

'No. I followed her up-town, to Berkeley Square. It's Simon Brand!'

For a moment, the name didn't register on Dodd. He stared at the phone stupidly. 'Who?'

Westerly said, 'Simon Brand. You know — the private detective . . . '

Todd swallowed. 'I know,' he said. His

60

brain raced. Brand. He'd read something about him in the papers recently — a sharp operator. He was getting in really deep now. 'All right, Don,' he said. 'I'll take it from here.' And he cradled the phone.

He tugged at his ear worriedly. He didn't want to tangle with Brand — not in person. He'd have to employ somebody. Who? Names and faces flicked through his mind. He had to get the girl away from Brand; scare her into the open again. Then he had to kill as quickly and efficiently as possible.

Scare her out . . .

Suddenly Gerald Dodd smiled. He was thinking of the ideal man for that job: Arnie the Ape, from Islington.

More confident now, Gerald Dodd picked up the phone again.

*　*　*

At seven thirty p.m. a red Porche swept along Knightsbridge and turned into Lowndes Square with Marla Dean at the wheel. The wet road reflected the light of

61

street-lamps, and a few pedestrians scurried past under umbrellas. It was a dismal evening but Doll Winters, seated beside Marla, felt as if she were travelling on her own private cloud.

She had eaten at a select restaurant in Piccadilly. Now she rode in a smart, sleekly-styled car. Life was very good for some, she thought wistfully, though she would have preferred cod-and-chips to plaice meunière.

Marla Dean parked outside a modern block of flats and both girls ducked through the rain and ran up the steps. A porter said, 'Evening, Miss Dean,' and they went up in the lift. Doll felt subdued as she walked behind Brand's slim, elegant secretary into her flat.

'Let me take your coat, Miss Winters,' Marla Dean said briskly. 'Just make yourself at home.'

Doll stared in open-mouthed admiration at the silver-grey walls, the pale lemon Venetian blinds, red roses in a crystal bowl. She felt it was not the sort of place where she could kick her shoes off and put her feet up. She wasn't used to this sort of room. It overawed her for a moment. But then . . .

Dorothea Winters, star of stage, screen and television, swept into her Mayfair luxury flat, shooed her admirers away, discarded a sable wrap, and . . .

'Please sit down,' Marla said softly. 'Try to relax.'

Doll perched stiffly on the edge of a chair as Brand's blonde secretary disappeared through a swing door into the kitchen. It wasn't fair, Doll thought again, looking hard at the red roses and even harder for a picture of Simon Brand. She couldn't see one.

Marla returned with a tray bearing a silver coffee pot and cups. 'It's early yet,' she said. 'Would you like to watch television?'

'I'd like to hear about Mr. Brand,' Doll returned promptly. 'Tell me about him. What's he really like?'

'Mr. Brand?' Marla Dean seemed to smile with her whole body. Her dark blue eyes sparkled like sunlight on tropical waters. 'He's — ' She had difficulty in finding words to do justice to the feeling Doll's innocent question had evoked.

'He's . . . he's my idea of a complete man,' she said simply.

She poured the coffee, handed Doll a cup. 'Once,' she said reminiscently, 'I was a frightened young woman myself — very fnghtened. Mr. Brand saved my life. So, you see, you needn't worry either. As soon as he gets back — '

But there her reassuring words came to an end abruptly.

For in that very instant, wood panelling splintered and the door crashed inwards. And a man filled the gap — a huge man, with long arms and a squat, unshaven face.

He looked like an ape with glaring eyes and sharp teeth.

Doll Winters screamed.

She screamed and she dropped her cup as the ape-like man came at her. She scrambled to her feet, and lunged sideways to evade his huge, grasping hands. Then she bolted.

They'd come for her! She ought to have known that they would!

Meantime Marla Dean launched herself at the intruder. She flung her arms around his neck and tried to drag him backwards as he pursued Doll. It was like trying to stop a runaway train. He took no notice of her at all.

Doll didn't pause to collect her coat or her suitcase. She raced through the bedroom and tore open a window. An iron fire escape went down into the darkness. Rain lashed at her as she stumbled down the ladder.

Marla Dean hammered the ape-like intruder with her fists, but he brushed her off as if she were no more than a troublesome mosquito. He started down the fire escape after Doll.

Marla Dean picked herself up, badly shaken. She stared out into the rain. It didn't look as though the ape-man was going to catch Doll. Doll Winters was travelling fast. Nevertheless, there was only one thing to do now, and Marla did it.

Whirling around swiftly she ran to the phone.

She dialled: nine, nine, nine.

* * *

One glimpse of Arnie the Ape had been enough for Doll Winters. She fled down the fire escape, shivering as heavy boots rattled the iron rungs behind her. In rain-streaked darkness, she reached the bottom of the ladder and ran along a short, dark alley to the brightly lit square.

There was no one about, only a black saloon car parked across the road. Doll swung in the opposite direction. Her sharp heels drummed a staccato tattoo on the pavement . . . and the black saloon car slid into motion and followed her slowly, discreetly, waiting for her to get beyond the bright lights.

Doll hurried along the Brompton Road, hugging lighted shop windows. She turned once, was that car following her? She began to run again, her heart thumping. She wasn't safe anywhere, she thought desperately. The police didn't believe her, and her own mother had turned her away. Now Mr. Brand's secretary had failed her. She was on her own, friendless and hunted by an implacable killer. She had to get away; find a place to hide.

She twisted round again, and looked back. As the following car passed a street lamp she caught a glimpse of a sad face under the brim of a bowler hat. It was him. She was sure of it now, and terror knifed through her afresh. She ran through the rain.

Ahead, a neon light blazed and music blared. The sign read: *El Torero*. Doll dived into the coffee bar like a ship seeking shelter from a storm. A solid beat of taxi-horn sax and amplified guitars blasted through a throng of colourful teenagers. Cigarette smoke hung in a cloud under fluorescent tubes. A Latin motif, the bullfight, was splashed in crimson on cream-painted walls.

Doll relaxed, pushing her way to the counter. She was safe for the moment — the killer couldn't do anything to her in here. And she'd tag along with this crowd when they left.

A boy whistled. 'Say, look't the mouse!' Narrowed eyes looked her over.

Doll sniffed and tugged down the tail

of her sweater — it was riding high again. She ignored them. 'Espresso,' she said to the counterman, and dug into her pocket for coins. She had only a few pounds, she realized in a panic — and her post office bank book was in the suitcase back in Marla Dean's flat. So now she was broke near enough . . .

A smooth, confident voice beside her said 'I'll get that for you, kid.'

Doll turned, saw a mouthful of teeth, a sharply pointed chin, a pair of hot, eager eyes. Their owner wore a green cord jacket with a spotted bow tie and felt waistcoat. She forced a smile. She had to stay inside this place — out of reach. And she thought she could handle the big bad wolf leering at her. 'Okay,' she murmured.

The man with the hot, eager eyes pushed through the crowd, and Doll followed him. They squeezed on to a low seat in a dim corner. 'I'm Harry,' he informed her. It was almost a boast.

He was thin, he was restless, and a muscle in his cheek twitched continuously. He seemed to be some kind of beatnik — but cleaner than most.

He snapped his fingers to the pulsing beat of the taxi-horn sax and guitars.

'I'm Harry,' he repeated. He tittered, and spittle drooled down his sharp-pointed chin.

His pupils were pinpoints. 'What's your handle, baby?'

'Doll,' she told him.

'Doll. Baby Doll! Hey, that's good!' He tittered again, and his cheek twitched, and he sang falsetto. 'I'm going to buy a Baby Doll that I can call my own, a doll that other fellas cannot steal — '

He was bursting with energy, forced out of him like sweat by some inner stimulus. Dope . . . ? Doll Winters wondered.

The air was hot in the coffee bar, and her damp clothes began to steam. She pushed back wet, bedraggled hair with one hand. Harry's eyes glittered, roving over her tight black skirt and her sweater. 'You've got something there, Doll,' he purred. 'Does a man good to see a well-stacked piece. I don't go for these straight up-and-down dames meself.'

Abruptly, he clamped a hand on her thigh.

Doll wriggled under the hand and managed to force it away. He grinned at her. 'Not here, huh?'

'That's right, Harry. Not here.'

'I got a car outside,' he offered. She didn't say anything.

The music changed to the latest hit, and Harry hummed the tune under his breath, beating time on her thigh with his fingers. She knew what he was up to: what she'd heard girls at the factory who'd been out with what soldiers call 'reconnaissance in depth'. But she put up with it for the moment.

Here in the coffee bar, at least there was warmth and a kind of gaiety — however spurious. Outside, death waited. She wondered briefly what had happened to Marla Dean. She remembered Arnie the Ape, and she shuddered.

'Cold baby?' Harry was breathing hot air m her face. 'Why don't you come back to my place and get out of those wet things?'

'I'm fine as I am,' Doll watched a

crowd of teenagers pile out through the door, wisecracking, calling 'goodnights, and pairing off. This might be a good time to leave, she thought. And with the man called Harry at least she'd be safe from the killer. 'All right,' she said. 'All right, Harry. Let's go.'

'Sure, kid. Anything you say.'

Outside the coffee bar, rain slanted down and the customers dispersed. Across the road a black Rover Saloon was parked, waiting. Doll clutched Harry's arm. 'Where's your car?'

'Farther on down the street, baby. Why?'

'There's a man over there — in that black saloon car. He's been bothering me. I want to shake him off.'

'Done as soon as said, kid.' Harry smiled. 'Not to worry at all. I'm gonna take good care of you . . . oh, yes . . . '

Hand tight on her arm, he walked her down the street to a battered Ford. He opened the door and pushed her inside, looking back with a frown. 'This heap don't seem much, Doll, but she can travel. We'll soon shake the car.'

He got in behind the wheel, and twisted the key in the ignition. He gunned the engine. As he moved out from the kerb he saw the black Rover Saloon swing out after him. 'So he wants to play, huh . . . ? All right, kid. Watch this!'

He stamped on the accelerator, and swung the wheel hard round. He roared into Ovington Square. He went round the square three times cornering like an expert at Le Mans and still the Rover Saloon stayed on his tail. Harry frowned into the rear mirror, his cheek twitching frenetically. 'Guy must be crazy.'

He rocketed out of the square, twisting and turning through back streets, working his way south to the river.

He let the Ford flat out along the Thames Embankment, overshot traffic lights and turned off, then turned sharply again into a dark, unlit mews. He cut both his engine and his lights simultaneously, and waited. Seconds later, the Rover Saloon flashed by . . .

'Lost him,' Harry grunted with satisfaction. 'Good! This is no time to have company hanging around.'

And he slid an arm round Doll's shoulders; edged closer. 'Just you and me now, baby,' he said softly.

Doll wrenched away and jerked open the car door. 'Thanks for the ride — '

His hand tightened on her; his voice hardened. 'You aren't leaving just yet, kid. I got you out of a jam, and you're going to say thanks. Now . . . give!'

As he pawed at her, Doll Winters shrank back. It seemed she had only escaped one load of trouble to bounce right into another.

By now, Doll Winters was fast beginning to wish that she'd never been born.

6

Out Of The Frying Pan . . .

Mr. Gerald Dodd, murderer, status recently acquired, eased his foot off the accelerator and peered through the twin arcs of wind-screen wipers into the rain-swept dark of Chelsea, S.W.3.

He'd lost Doll Winters, and he felt depressed as he circled the maze of streets sandwiched between Kings Road and the Thames Embankment. Somehow, somewhere, Doll Winters and the character in the old Ford had given him the slip. By now, they could be driving fast out of town in an unknown direction, or they could be shacked up for the night in any one of the hundreds of shadowy houses surrounding him.

He breathed hard, reversed and coasted round, watching the side turnings.

A police car passed him and uniformed men stared out at him. They didn't stop.

Dodd sweated. He thought: Get the hell out of this! He pulled into the kerb by a public call box, and ducked through the rain. He grabbed up the phone and pushed coins into the slot, and dialled.

He waited impatiently for Westerly, his garage foreman, to come on at the other end of the line, and then snapped: 'Get Arnie the Ape under cover, and keep him under cover! And, Don, pass the word to find a second-hand Ford,' he gave the number, and added: 'It was outside *El Torero* in Brompton Road, and I lost it somewhere in Chelsea The driver picked up our girl . . . '

He uttered only a few sentences more, then he put down the phone and returned to his car. And, starting up the engine again, he scowled. He'd scared the Winters girl away from Brand only to lose her. He sucked on an indigestion tablet. It was something, he thought, to have the use of a network designed for picking up cars. He'd get the word — and that young man would talk.

He'd lead him straight to the girl . . . or else God help him!

Harry's twitching face loomed over her, a white moon of tension. There was a glitter in his feverish eyes that she didn't like. She pushed his hands away and said, 'Lay off — you've picked the wrong girl for that game.'

'Aw, c'mon kid,' he urged. 'A little slap and tickle never hurt anyone.'

Doll wriggled along the seat towards the open car door, and swung one nyloned leg out into the rain. He tried to kiss her, one hand pulling at her. She dropped her head and sank sharp teeth into the roving hand. Harry jerked back, swearing. 'You little bitch!'

She ducked out of the car, cannoned into a wall in the dark and staggered off-balance. She heard him behind her, yelling: 'You're not running out on me like that!'

He was on top of her.

She felt his hands on her. He dragged her back to the car, jerked open the rear door; started to force her inside. And then an imperative voice suddenly boomed out of nowhere: 'Take your filthy hands off her!'

Looking up through the rain, Doll glimpsed a bulky figure looming out of the night. A hefty stick thudded across Harry's shoulders, and he squealed. Again, the stick came down. 'Let her go, I say!'

Harry turned to ward off another blow, and Doll wriggled clear. She leant against a wall, dizzy and panting. Her rescuer, garbed in a shiny black mackintosh, belaboured Harry until he scrambled into his car and drove off at high speed.

Doll gasped out: 'Thanks!'

'Where's your rubber mac, child?' the voice boomed at her. A face loomed up close, and Doll saw with some shock that the booming voice belonged to a woman: a very masculine woman.

'Where's your rubber mac? Don't say you haven't got one! Nothing like a rubber mac in this weather . . . see how the folds ripple and gleam? Imported from Paris — nothing like it over here!'

The masculine woman's face floated like a grotesque, painted mask in front of

Doll's eyes. 'Where do you live, child?'

Doll Winters shivered suddenly. She realized she was soaked to the skin, standing in the pouring rain with nowhere to go — an implacable killer hunting her. She said in a small voice: 'I — I don't have a place at the moment.'

'Then come with me, child!'

Doll followed the owner of the booming voice. She had to run to keep up with her rescuer's giant strides. A door opened in a wall, and they went through a garden and up some steps to the porch of an expensive-looking house.

And there a key turned in a lock, and yellow light blazed out as a door opened, and Doll saw that her rescuer was a heavily-built woman of about forty, dressed in gleaming black mackintosh, and riding boots, and carrying a thick, steel-shod walking stick. Her face was coated with thickly-applied make-up . . . Doll was fascinated.

'Come inside, child. You may call me Miss Margaret.'

Doll advanced after Miss Margaret across a wall-to-wall fitted carpet and into a long room where an ornate chandelier threw warm light over red plush and heavy antique furniture. A three-bar electric fire burned in an open grate.

'Stand in front of the fire,' Miss Margaret ordered, 'and get out of those wet clothes before you take pneumonia!' She dropped her heavy stick in a chair and shed her mackintosh. Doll stared at a tightly corseted caricature of Mae West . . . then the astonishing Miss Margaret went into another room and returned with a towel. 'Rub yourself dry, child, while I find you something to wear.'

When she next returned, Miss Margaret handed Doll a schoolgirl's gym tunic. It was too small for her and fitted her tightly finishing three inches above her knees. Doll was glad the girls at the factory could not see her now. She felt ridiculous.

'Very smart, my dear,' boomed Miss Margaret approvingly. 'It suits you! It belongs to my niece, but she won't mind you borrowed it. She's away at school.' She took up Doll's wet clothes. 'I'll put these to dry. You must stay here tonight.

Tomorrow I'll want to know all about you. I'm interested in you, child, very interested. And now we'll eat ... ' she brought two bowls and set them down on a solid oak table.

'Sit down,' she ordered.

Doll drew up a chair and gazed into her bowl. It must be soup she thought wildly, trying hard not to shudder. The steaming liquid was a hideous purple, and things like lumps of jellied fat floated in it. Revolting!

'Health food,' Miss Margaret explained briefly. 'Eat up — it'll do you a power of good.'

Doll didn't dare to refuse. There was something overpowering, even frightening, about her hostess. She forced herself to finish the soup. The next course was chopped raw carrot sprinkled with grated cheese.

'D'you — you eat like this all the time?' Doll mumbled.

'Of course! Finest food in the world,' Miss Margaret assured her, fitting a black Russian cigarette into a long ebony holder. 'I hope you haven't started to smoke yet. Children shouldn't.'

'I don't smoke,' Doll admitted.

'Capital. Now, come, and I'll show you to your room.'

They went up narrow, carpeted stairs, one flight and then another. What an oddly-shaped house, Doll thought, very long and narrow, and very tall. She seemed to go on climbing forever . . . now they were going up bare, creaking boards. To an attic, she supposed.

They came to a narrow landing, dust covered, the paper peeling off the walls.

'In here,' Miss Margaret rasped, throwing open a door. Doll walked in. A single naked light bulb revealed a bed, a chair, wooden floorboards. The only window had been bricked up.

'Sleep well, my dear — tomorrow we must have a nice long chat.' Doll saw a cunning smirk on the painted face, and then Miss Margaret was gone, slamming the door behind her.

Doll heard bolts shoot home on the far side. The light in the room abruptly went out. In utter darkness, Doll Winters stood completely bewildered; frightened;

wondering what she had walked into.

Had she jumped out of the frying pan into the fire?

Harry, her pick-up in the coffee bar, had at least been a simple and elemental, down-to-earth soul — despite his twitches. But this woman, Miss Margaret, was quite outside Doll's experience.

7

. . . Into The Fire

'After I called the police,' Marla Dean said. 'I stayed close to the phone in case Doll Winters rang back. After all, she'd left both her suitcase and coat in my flat, and it was pouring with rain. That ape went after her — and I'm glad he didn't come back — but it would surprise me if he caught up with her. She was moving fast . . . '

Marla Dean was in Simon Brand's private room in the office suite, which overlooked Berkeley Square. So was Brand himself — together with his young partner, Nick Chandler. Bright morning sunlight slanted in through the windows. Outside, the plane trees shed their leaves carpeting the square golden-brown, glistening in the aftermath of the rain.

'I went through her things then,' Marla continued, 'and found a post office bank book. She wouldn't have much money on her I'd say, so she can't have gone far. But she never rang me back.'

Simon Brand and Nick Chandler had driven through the night from the West Country. They both looked tired and travel-stained. Brand sat behind his broad desk, smoking, preoccupied. He had played back the tape Marla had made and heard Doll Winters tell her own story. For him it held the clear ring of truth.

He was angry. The Winters girl had come to him for help, and now she was on the run with a killer after her . . .

'You did the right thing, Marla,' he said. 'It was just unfortunate that the ape, as you call him, burst in and scared her.'

'He scared me, too,' Marla admitted. 'He handled me as though I were a mere cobweb.' She rubbed her bruises tenderly.

Brand's blue-grey eyes hardened. He disapproved of strange men bursting into his secretary's flat with malice aforethought. It was a procedure he intended to discourage just as soon as he caught up with this so-called 'ape'. He said, 'Send me a bill for the damage, Marla.'

In the background, another man cleared his throat.

This was Deputy-Commander Leonard Walford of New Scotland Yard, an old friend of Brand's. Grey-haired and rather military-looking, he gestured with the straight stem of his pipe. 'Patrol cars covered the area as soon as Marla here contacted me,' he said. 'The men on the beat were alerted. But we couldn't find this character who burst into Miss Dean's flat, and we couldn't find the Winters girl. Both had vanished completely.' He glanced at Marla. 'But we don't have to worry about this character you've called 'The Ape' — he's harmless enough.'

'So I gathered,' Marla returned dryly. 'I liked the harmless way he smashed my door. I saw him in action — remember?'

'He is harmless, though,' Walford insisted. 'I recognize him from your description. He used to be a wrestler. You know — one of the grunt-and-groan 'all-in' boys. He only looks dangerous. He wouldn't hurt a fly really. His name's Arnie Bendix. He does odd jobs for small-time crooks these days. Anything requiring brawn and no brain.'

'But he scared Miss Winters into the open where a killer could get at her,' Brand said tersely. 'You've got to pull him in and find out who paid for the job.'

Walford nodded his iron-grey head. 'I've been on to Tooting. They've checked with Doll Winters's landlady, and someone did break in there. It looks like murder all right . . . This man called Gillespie was known to be a car thief in a small way, and he may have had a run in with one of the big boys. The stolen car racket's been building up for years . . . and it's getting more and more organized. That's what's got us worried. Maybe this case will give us the break that we need.'

Brand spoke bluntly. 'I'm not interested in car-stealing, Len. It's the girl I'm thinking about — she's in real danger. And I feel responsible for her . . . after all, it was me she came to for help.'

'We're doing all we can,' Walford said.

Brand stubbed out his cigarette. 'I'm going to ask the *Daily Post* to run the story across their front page. Their chief reporter is a friend of mine. Tell Miss Winters to come in for protection — and I'll offer a reward for information. Can you fix it with the BBC and the Commercial boys to give it a news spot on both vision and sound?'

'Okay. If you say so.'

'Yes,' Brand said firmly. 'Doll Winters is the one person who can identify the killer. The sooner she reports to a police station, assured that her story will be believed, the better it's going to be.'

Walford rose. 'Hope your hunch is right. I'll get on with it.'

'Nick,' Brand said briskly, addressing his young partner, 'I want you to comb the south side of the river. Start at Tooting. You're looking for a lead to a garage handling stolen cars.'

'Right, chief!'

Walford frowned. 'That's a pretty slender hope.'

Brand nodded. 'But the crashed blue Mini was taken from the South Bank and ended up in Tooting. The murder has all the earmarks of being planned by someone who knows the area . . . find me that man, Nick! A man who has a long, sad face underneath a bowler hat.'

Nick Chandler left the office.

'And you, Marla,' Simon Brand said to his secretary, 'I want you to go back to your flat. Doll Winters may return. Marilyn and Miss Rington can handle things here at the office. I'm going to work with the police and cover the area around Lowndes Square again.

'We've got to find Doll Winters before the killer does!'

★   ★   ★

She was the kidnapped heiress of a Texan oil multi-millionaire, and the sinister gangster figure standing over her snarled 'We'll collect half a million bucks ransom, or . . . '

Doll Winters's dream ended abruptly at the sound of a bolt being withdrawn on the far side of the door, and the nightmare, temporarily held in abeyance, flooded back. She blinked as the door was flung open and daylight hit her eyes.

Miss Margaret stood there, a smile

creasing her garishly painted face. 'A lovely morning, my dear,' she boomed. 'I trust you slept well? Here are your shoes and stockings — they're dry now. You must come down, breakfast is waiting. The bathroom is on the floor below . . . '

Doll Winters, late of Levinson Structural Steel Fabrications Limited, stared hard at this solidly-engineered woman dressed completely in black. Miss Margaret's figure was tightly corseted; her fingers encrusted with rings. Fantastic pendants hung glittering from her ears. She looked a freak — but hardly dangerous in the morning light. Doll's earlier fears began to evaporate. Perhaps she would stay here a while. At least she was safe from the killer . . .

'I'll be down as soon as I've washed,' Doll said. She reached for her nylons and flimsy stiletto heels.

'That's right, child. Cleanliness is next to godliness. And don't forget behind the ears!'

Miss Margaret went downstairs slowly, and Doll washed in the bathroom. She struggled into her gym tunic, sure something would split at any moment. It was so tight she was almost afraid to take a breath, and her shapely stockinged legs were extensively displayed beneath the ultra-short hemline.

Doll went downstairs to the long living room with its red plush and its antique furniture. Miss Margaret was seated at the table. 'I'd like my own clothes, please,' Doll said. 'After all, I'm not a schoolgirl!'

Miss Margaret appeared faintly disturbed by the request. 'There's no hurry, surely? They're . . . they're not quite dry yet. And you look charming, my dear. Now do eat up your fruit and nuts, and drink down your milk!'

Doll sat down, wishing it were fried bacon and eggs. 'And now tell me all about yourself,' the odd Miss Margaret said with a smirk of red-rouged lips.

Doll began, 'I'm hiding from a murderer . . . '

Mascaraed eyes boggled as she told all that had happened to her. 'My dear child, how terrible for you . . . but how thrilling! You simply must stay here. I insist on looking after you. Positively insist. My friends will be delighted, I know!'

'Your friends?'

'Of course — you don't know — how could you?' Miss Margaret became effusive. 'They'll just *love* you! You'll join our little circle and become one of us . . . it's just a small intimate group, really quite cosy when you get to know our little ways. We call ourselves the Physologists. I must admit we might seem a little . . . well . . . *odd* . . . .at first, but you'll soon grow into it, I do assure you.'

The grotesque painted mask beamed a smile. 'We Physologists have the most daring, exciting parties, dressing up, loads of make-up and jewellery and long hair. Simply everything! Very smart and fashionable . . . I think a French Maid's outfit might be just the thing for you, and you could wait at table, too. Servants are so slovenly these days, and there's noting nicer than a starched white collar — '

Doll Winters listened dumbfounded, uneasiness stirring within her as Miss Margaret spoke excitedly.

'Yes, yes, the French maid's outfit

. . . *très chic* . . . and Professor McIntyre will love that. You have just the figure, child. You'd love to dress up for us, wouldn't you?'

'I'm not sure that I would,' Doll mumbled. 'And who is Professor McIntyre?'

'McIntyre? One of us, my dear, one of our little circle. We're all keen physologists, you know. Some like one thing, some like another — but we get along pretty well together . . . '

Doll stared at her. Miss Margaret is mad, she thought numbly. Stark, raving mad. She'd get out of this house as fast as she could.

Miss Margaret swept on, quite carried away by her enthusiasm. 'And the dear horses! We have our own carriage and pair, and you can't imagine the thrill of driving a pair with their heads and mouths rigidly controlled by tight reins — '

'Are you kidding?' Doll burst out. 'Why, it sounds downright cruel!'

Miss Margaret's lips clamped shut. She looked at Doll with angry, gleaming eyes.

A chill ran down Doll's spine, and she pushed back her chair and stood up. 'I'm leaving,' she said hurriedly.

'But you can't, my dear. I won't let you,' Miss Margaret purred.

'You see, I anticipated that you might be difficult, and took the precaution of locking all the doors and windows!' She, too, rose from the table. 'Really, the younger generation . . . simply no gratitude . . . and offered such a splendid opportunity!'

She crossed the room with determined strides, and snatched down a heavy riding whip from the wall. She turned to face Doll; glared at her.

'Now, my girl, we'll see about disciplining you!'

Miss Margaret flicked her wrist, and the whiplash cracked. Doll Winters backed away. 'You're — you're barmy!' she gasped.

★   ★   ★

Don Westerly, Dodd's garage foreman, stood outside the *Continental Strippery*

93

in a garlic-scented street behind Shaftesbury Avenue, admiring a selection of glossy pin-ups.

There was one piece, a slant-eyed Chinese miss holding crossed fans in front of her. Don Westerly fancied her. He wouldn't mind getting to know her, he thought, and his imagination ran riot for a few seconds.

Westerly was unmarried. He preferred variety: a different girl each time. And on the sort of money he was making with Dodd he could afford to indulge his taste.

Arnie the Ape had been taken care of. He was out of town where no one would find him in a hurry. Now Westerly waited for the Ford to arrive. According to information received, Harry Hodges, the junkie who owned the Ford, made a habit of dropping in at the *Strippery's* bar during the lunch-hour for a drink, a peep, and a sandwich.

Time passed pleasantly enough for Don Westerly, viewing the pin-ups. He glanced at his watch from time to time, and then he nodded. Any minute now.

And, as he turned, an old Ford drove up and parked.

Westerly checked the number-plate — this was the one — and studied the driver. A pointed chin, gleaming white teeth, cord jacket, and bowtie. This Harry Hodges wouldn't be hard to handle, Westerly thought and darted a quick look up and down the street to see who was about.

Harry came twitching across the pavement and made to move around Westerly to get into the club. Westerly laid a big, tattooed hand on his arm. 'Mr. Harry Hodges?' he inquired politely.

'What's it to you?' Harry was taken aback. He saw a stocky man in a raincoat, his eyes differently coloured, lending him a menacing aspect. Not the police, he decided, and relaxed visibly.

Reading his thoughts, Westerly smiled. 'If you're Hodges I can put an easy hundred your way . . . '

'I'm Hodges.' Harry said quickly. 'Let's go into the bar. We can talk there. I'm a member, you're my guest. Okay?'

'Okay,' Westerly agreed easily.

The photographic prints lining the passage inside the club were of a more intimate nature than those outside, and the peroxided barmaid had a low line in decolletage. 'What'll it be?' Westerly asked.

'Double whisky.'

'And a rum for me.'

They drank, and Harry Hodges looked coolly at him. 'Well what's the easy money?'

'A friend of mine is looking for a girl,' Westerly said quietly. 'A girl wearing a red sweater, tight black skirt and stiletto-heeled shoes. You picked her up at the *El Torero* in Knightsbridge last night.'

Harry tensed, his face sickly. If someone had laid a complaint . . . He swallowed the rest of his whisky, thrust the empty glass blindly down at the counter and swung away. Westerly gripped his arm — hard. 'Don't know what you're talking about,' Harry mumbled.

'You know all right,' Westerly said. 'Hell, I don't care what happened between you. You can talk. All my friend wants is to find the girl. Now, where is she?'

Harry Hodges's cheek muscle twitched faster than ever. 'I don't know — '

Westerly's expression became as bleak as a winter sky. His hand tightened till Harry Hodges winced. 'We can beat it out of you . . . but we like to do things in a friendly way.' He laid two fifty-pound notes on the counter and covered them with one big hand. 'They're yours when you've finished talking.'

From the corner of his eye, he watched a girl come into the bar, the slant-eyed Chinese girl whose picture he had been admiring outside. And she looked even better in the flesh. Her cheongsam, tightly drawn about her slim body, gaped open as she swung on to a stool, to reveal long and very slim legs. Westerly swallowed hard. From that glimpse it looked as if she'd come straight off the stage.

His voice roughened. 'Hurry it up, Hodges! I've got other business to see to!'

'I don't know where she is. Honest! She wasn't any good. She ran out on me.'

'Where was this? Spill it!'

Harry Hodges said: 'I parked in a mews leading off Chelsea Manor Street, near the Embankment. The first turning on the left — you can't miss it. The little bitch ran out on me. Some damn woman showed up and I had to beat it. I don't know what happened after that. I got the hell out of it.'

'This woman who showed up — she interfered? In the mews?'

Harry nodded sullenly. 'The stupid old crow started laying into me with a ruddy big stick!'

Westerly said thoughtfully: 'If she found you in the mews, it's likely she lives thereabouts. What did she look like?'

'It was raining, and I didn't get too good a look. But she wore a black slicker . . . a big woman she was . . . with a voice like a foghorn. All made up. Heavily.'

Westerly considered this information. 'All right,' he decided. 'We'll find her.'

He took his hand off the money on the counter.

Harry Hodges grabbed it, thrust the two notes into his pocket and hurried out. He didn't know what it was all about, and he didn't want to know. Harry Hodges was a great boy for keeping his nose clean . . .

Don Westerly turned and stared at the Chinese stripper. She gave him a big smile. His mouth went dry just looking at her. His voice thickened. 'I've got to make a phone call — I'll be five minutes. Understand? You wait for me here. Okay?'

The Chinese girl nodded.

8

Fire!

Brand had been pounding the pavement for hours, doing his own legwork. He covered a small, tight area round Lowndes Square, checking every place Doll Winters might have gone, or where she might have been noticed. He had no lead so far.

There was a pantherish quality in his approach, in the set of his jaw and the way that he moved. He would not give up the search. Somewhere, there was the lead that he needed. Someone must have seen the girl he was looking for. The fact that she had come to him for help needled him to a relentless pursuit.

He started down the Brompton Road, beginning a long routine check of shops, offices and private houses, and finally reached *El Torero*. He almost passed it by. In daylight, it was a restaurant catering mainly for businessmen . . . and then Brand visualized it by night, neon flaring, music blaring. A coffee bar. Just the sort of place Doll Winters would feel familiar with, and the sort of place that she'd enter.

He entered too, then, and passed between crowded tables and walls adorned with scenes of the bullring to reach the counter. He showed his identification and a photograph of Doll Winters: a snapshot that the Tooting police had dug out in a hurry. He asked the counterman, 'Were you on duty last night?'

'Yeah. Last night, tonight, and every night,' the counterman said tiredly, and straightened. There was something about Brand's blue-grey eyes that pulled him out of his tiredness and sharpened his wits.

'Did you notice this girl?' Brand tapped the photograph with a lean finger, watching the man's face intently. 'She was wearing a tight black skirt and a red sweater. She'd have been wet and breathless. A little pale, too, maybe.'

'Yeah now, that's right . . . I remember her . . . nice little chick, good figure . . . she was in here last night.'

Simon Brand experienced a deep feeling of relief. The tension that had been building up inside him began to slacken. This was the break.

'When she left, was she with anyone?'

The counterman rubbed the side of his jaw. 'There was quite a crowd in, mostly regulars. I don't think they knew her — and I hadn't seen her before myself . . . yeah now, that's right, the one they call Harry picked her up. I bet he made the most of it, knowing Harry. I remember, they went out together, and she was hanging on to his arm like he was a life-saver . . . '

I'll bet she was, Brand thought grimly. A case of any port in a storm.

The counterman grinned. 'Nice for Harry! She was a real looker. I remember she had very good legs, too. And — ' His hands made motions in the air.

Brand said: 'Where can I find this Harry? What's his surname? Do you know where he lives?'

'Sorry I can't help you there. Harry's just a casual . . . ' The counterman paused to fill two glass cups from his espresso machine.

'He might drop in a couple of times a week, then I mightn't see him for two, three weeks at a time. Think he's on the weed. I doubt if the regular gang know much about him either.'

'Can you describe him?'

The counterman tried, and Brand listened carefully and wrote down a description of Harry the Junk in a notebook. Then he went to the telephone and called New Scotland Yard. This was a job for Walford's organization. It was going to take time to find Harry, and time was the one thing he didn't have. Not with a killer on the girl's tail.

* * *

For a long moment, Doll Winters froze, watching the heavy riding whip in Miss Margaret's jewelled hand with the fascination of a rabbit watching a snake. Her fingers scrabbled at the wall behind her.

Then the thong hissed down . . .

The lash cut through the thin gym tunic into Doll's shoulder, and she cried out. Desperately, she flung herself forward, one small fist driving for the older woman's painted face. Miss Margaret cursed and raised the whip again. 'Brat!' she snarled. 'Ungrateful brat!'

Doll turned and ran. There was only one way of escape left to her — up the stairs. She went up, fast, with Miss Margaret panting behind her and the lash flicking her ankles. 'I'll tame your spirit, child!'

Doll Winters kept going. She wasn't thinking clearly. She only wanted to get away from the mad woman with the whip . . . and before she fully realized it, she was on the top floor, the floor with one room, where she'd been imprisoned before. She was trapped!

Doll Winters darted into the room and looked around wildly. There was no way out — and the only door locked on the outside. She began to tremble.

Miss Margaret, breathing heavily, arrived in the doorway. She stood there, staring at Doll, flicking her whip. 'I'll teach you a lesson, my girl — you'll stay in your room on bread and water . . . until this evening. Tonight the circle meets.' She bared her teeth in a ferocious smile. 'Discipline is what you need, child, and I don't doubt that Professor McIntyre will have a notion of how to tame you!'

She slammed and bolted the door and Doll was a prisoner once again — locked up in the dark with her fears.

★   ★   ★

'Here, boss,' Westerly called softly. He stood in a recessed gateway in the high brick wall running along one side of a Chelsea mews. It was late evening, dark, with no street lamp to break up the shadows.

Gerald Dodd, dressed in dark topcoat and scarf, bowler hat jammed down lightly on his head, joined him. 'Any sign of the girl?'

'No, but I've spotted the woman Harry Hodges told me about. She lives opposite.

Bit queer in the head, if you ask me, all dolled up like an ageing Mae West. Seems like she's throwing a party . . . three taxis rolled up half-an-hour ago.'

Westerly spat out the remnants of an unlit cigarette. 'And — the types, boss! Odd balls, every one of 'em. What the hell goes on inside? Any idea? It's got me beat. You still figure the girl's in there?'

Gerald Dodd scowled. 'Where else? She's got to be in there . . . ' His face was beaded with cold sweat. Only an hour ago he had been watching television. There was a call out for Doll Winters, asking her to report to the nearest police station; advising anyone who saw her to telephone New Scotland Yard. He had to get to her fast.

'If she's inside, we'll soon have her out — and finish her!'

His hand closed about the gun in his pocket. A heavy .45 calibre revolver; loaded. He didn't like the idea . . . shuddered as he thought of warm, shattered flesh . . . but he was desperate now.

'My car's parked round the corner, Don. The stuff's in the boot. Get it.'

Westerly moved off silently, a shadow in the night-darkness. He found the Rover Saloon and opened the boot. He smelt oil. There was a sack, filled with something soft, and he carried it back to the mews.

'Come on,' Dodd grunted, and crossed to the gate leading to Miss Margaret's house. He opened the gate and they crossed a dark garden, feet crunching on a gravel path.

No light showed through the heavy red curtains ahead. The house appeared silent and deserted. 'I wonder what sort of fun and games goes on inside,' Westerly muttered. 'Maybe we're doing that kid a favour . . . '

Gerald Dodd went up to the front porch, and waited. Westerly went to the side of the house, and felt along the wall for a ventilator. He found one, set low down in the wall.

He emptied the sack, and packed old, oil-soaked rags round the ventilator.

Then he struck a match and applied the tiny flame to the rags. The oil caught, the rags smouldered. A dense cloud of choking black smoke rose and billowed. Westerly backed off, coughing.

Gerald Dodd waited for the air to fill with smoke. Then he hammered on the door, and shouted: 'Fire . . . fire!'

★   ★   ★

Little Doll Winters had heard a bolt being drawn back.

She swung her legs off the bed and sat up, tense and expectant. What now, she wondered.

The door opened slowly, and light shone in from the passage beyond. The weird Miss Margaret came into the room — and Doll saw a man just behind her.

She stared at him blankly. He might have been an actor straight off the stage after playing in some Regency drama. He wore a brocaded jacket with heavy cuffs, knee breeches and silken stockings. And there were silver buckles on his shoes.

Doll checked a nervous laugh, relieved to see that Miss Margaret was not carrying her riding whip. She had been lying in pitch blackness for hours, waiting.

'Stand up, child,' Miss Margaret rapped. 'Let Professor McIntyre take a good look at you.'

Doll Winters rose slowly, looking for a chance to bolt past them and race down the stairs. But they blocked the doorway.

Professor McIntyre was a wizen-faced, yellow-skinned old man with sparse blue-black hair whose colour had run in places on to his ochrous scalp. He stared at Doll's long, shapely legs and sucked his ill-fitting dentures. 'A sweet child,' he said with enthusiasm. 'And the tunic suits her to perfection. I do congratulate you, Margaret!'

'But recalcitrant. Definitely recalcitrant.'

'Ah . . . that must be checked,' Professor McIntyre murmured. But certainly!'

'Downstairs, girl!' Miss Margaret boomed at Doll. 'Unless you expect the Professor to carry you. The Physologist circle is waiting.'

Doll thought about it. Perhaps this

madwoman would be better with her friends around — and she didn't want him touching her. She walked past them, down the stairs. Voices whispered excitedly when she entered the long living room. Heavy crimson curtains were draped round the walls and the light was subdued. Doll's nostrils twitched. Incense was burning.

Doll remembered the smell of incense from her High Church days as a schoolgirl in Balham. Every Friday, she and her classmates had all walked crocodile fashion, from their Church of England School to Saint Cuthbert's just off Balham High Street. And, at Saint Cuthbert's where the soft candle-shine and the scent of incense and the voices of priest and choir all climbed up to mingle in the echoing vaults of the ancient roof, Doll's schoolgirl heart had discovered a strange kind of peace.

Strange, that is, to her. For though her mother continually insisted on describing herself as 'religious' and 'respectable' yet there was little of the peace of God to be found in her home.

The fact was that ever since Doll's father had first just unaccountably vanished out of her life, and then, later, been reported by her mother as dead the atmosphere at home had become ever more and more embittered. Doll couldn't think why. And, always, her mother had used the words 'religious' and 'respectable' like a pair of bludgeons.

'*I'm a religious woman, and I won't stand for no goings on from you, me gel! If you can't get in at a respectable time, you can get out and stay out for good!*

'*You're getting more and more like your father every day. And that's nothing to be proud of! You're going to the bad, just like him. You've got his blood in you. Him and his fancy tarts! But I'm not having it, see? You'll behave yourself, or clear off. I'm a religious woman, and this is a respectable house.*'

This had been the refrain all through Doll's adolescence, until Doll had finally taken her mother at her word, and had gone.

Still she remembered Saint Cuthbert's though, and recalled the strange kind of peace she had found there, and the sense of 'belonging'.

But the incense she smelt now, as she entered the long, crimson-draped living room in Miss Margaret's house, evoked no such sensations or feelings of peace.

This room held an unhealthy atmosphere . . .

Doll saw grotesque statues sitting around on high-backed, antique chairs — and then realized that they were not statues but people wearing unusual clothes, many faces heavy with make-up, others hideously masked.

Doll dragged in a breath.

Then — 'Darling!' an aged crone with a feather boa and six-inch heels tottered towards her and made to lay a wavering hand on her. 'Darling, you're sweet.'

'Don't be greedy, Agatha!' Miss Margaret rapped, and brushed the wavering hand aside, returning it to its owner. 'You always were one to hog new members of our little circle.'

'But I haven't had a new member for ages!' the old crone called Agatha pouted. 'I feel ripe for a little new blood.'

What were they, Doll wondered wildly. Vampires?

Miss Margaret was at her elbow — urging her forward. 'Parade yourself, child.'

Doll wheeled on her, 'I will not!'

'Disciplining, that's what she needs,' the man called Professor McIntyre murmured in the background. His unblinking gaze lingered over Doll. He sucked at his ill-fitting teeth. 'Disciplining first. Then the initiation . . . '

'Who's greedy now?' the feather-boaed Agatha cried. Her shrivelled chin wagged. 'You're always wanting to discipline people. You — '

Doll saw her chance.

No one was looking at her, not even the Professor now. She swung around; ran.

Professor McIntyre made a belated grab for her, but she twisted out of his reach. There was sudden uproar all around her as she streaked across the room. Then someone stuck out a foot and she tripped, and sprawled headlong on the thick pile of the carpet. 'Got you — !' Professor McIntyre pounced.

But, at that moment, a thunderous hammering sounded on the front door, and a muffled voice shouted: 'Fire . . . *fire!*' And Professor McIntyre paused, dentures gaping.

Then the aged crone called Agatha sniffed the air delicately. 'I do smell something . . . ' she said. And Miss Margaret wrenched open the door and smoke streamed in from the passage.

She ran to the front door; unlocked it; dragged it open. A dense cloud of oily black smoke immediately enveloped her, and made her cough and cover her mouth as she staggered back. 'Fire!' she called huskily. 'Get out, everybody!'

Panic flared in the long, crimson-draped room. The Physologists stampeded. The old crone called Agatha could be heard crying: 'Let me out! Let me out! My clairvoyant warned me! I won't be burned to death! I won't!'

There was a wild rush, and bodies jammed in the narrow passage.

Doll Winters was completely forgotten. She slipped like an eel from Professor McIntyre's grasp and joined the others in the rush to the door.

She ran along the passage into a pall of smoke. She saw a smart black overcoat with an expensive fur collar on a stand in the hall, and snatched it up as she passed. Despite her fear she realized the inadequacy of her attire.

She shrugged into the coat as she ran blindly out of the house . . .

★ ★ ★

Gerald Dodd stood well back from the smoke, waiting for her His gloved hand held his ex-Army revolver.

His foreman, Westerly, had returned to the car, and sat with the engine running, ready for a quick getaway.

Dodd watched the front door open and, seconds later, the Physologists poured from the house. Men in strange clothes and women with painted masks for faces rushed past him, unheeding, intent only upon escape. He stared like a hawk into the smoke — damn it, Westerly had overdone the smokescreen — looking for a young girl wearing a bright red sweater and tight black skirt.

He didn't see one.

He did notice a young woman in a smart black coat with fur-trimmed collar. She ran by with the others. She was ten yards away before Dodd suddenly swore and did an astonished double take. It was the girl he'd been waiting for. He hadn't expected her to be dressed up like that!

He lunged after her, charging over the garden, throwing up his gun hand as he ran, desperate for a shot at her. She darted through the gate and turned into the mews. Dodd reached the gate. Ahead, in the dark unlit mews he saw a shadowy figure fleeing before him and heard the clatter of high-heeled shoes. And Gerald Dodd knew from experience just how fast this girl could run.

His finger tightened on the trigger of his gun. It was madness, but he had to risk a shot. The explosion smashed out, shattering the quietness of the night. The bullet careened off a brick post at the corner of the mews as the girl turned into the street.

Startled painted faces swung round to

stare. A loud voice brayed: 'Really, there's no need for that!' And then Dodd, a stout man wearing a bowler hat and a mournful expression, crashed through the ranks of the Physologists, waving his gun.

They shouted at him as he shouldered them out of the way. An old crone with a feather boa threatened him with a hatpin. Gerald Dodd ignored them all. It was the girl that he wanted.

He reached the corner, and saw her passing beneath a street lamp.

He fired again wildly as he ran in pursuit.

9

Sanctuary

The crash of the gunshot terrified Doll. She shuddered as she heard the high-pitched whine of the bullet. As it sped past her to ricochet on a wall post, she turned the corner, running hard. She ran for her life. One glance back and a glimpse of a sad-faced man in a bowler hat was enough. She came close to breaking several Olympic records as she darted across the road and raced along a side street.

The killer had been waiting for her! Her heart pounded like a drum at the knowledge. The icy fingers of death seemed to clutch at her shoulder. The street was dark and deserted and she heard his footsteps echoing behind. The gun crashed again. A bullet screamed off the pavement, missing her by yards. But, to Doll Winters, it seemed very close indeed.

She kept running until the sound of pursuit was lost behind her. She had outdistanced the killer — but for how long? She swung round another corner into another street, breath sawing frantically through her throat. In the gloom she saw a high wall and leapt at it, fingers clawing for the top. She dragged herself up and dropped over; dropped on to grass and ran between shadowy elms towards a square, grey stone building.

There was a warped oaken door, partly open, and she squeezed through into a dusky interior. She stopped abruptly as she found herself confronted by an altar where two candles burned . . .

She sensed peace in the musty air, a still calmness remote from the nightmare haunting her. Memories of school days came flooding back. She fell on her knees before the altar. She fixed her eyes on the cross and prayed as she had never prayed before.

Doll Winters had found sanctuary.

Gerald Dodd paused, hesitating, at a street corner. A line of sweat creased his forehead. Which way had the girl gone? He peered into the darkness, turning this way and that and mouthing curses. The service revolver was heavy in his hand, dragging his arm down. He hadn't realized how heavy it was, and the shock of the explosions had numbed his wrist.

He was getting old, out of condition, and his topcoat hampered his movements. He hadn't a chance of catching up with the girl now. Damn, damn, damn! He'd lost her again . . . all on account of that large, unfamiliar coat she was wearing.

He heard a swish of tyres on the road and a black Rover Saloon braked hard beside him, door swinging open. Don Westerly leaned out, his face tense. 'The cops, boss! And that Brand — right on our heels! We've got to beat it, fast!'

Dodd deliberated for a moment only. He didn't know where the girl was, and had no time to hunt for her now. He'd have to put out another call — someone might spot her. It was his only chance.

The urgent blast of a police whistle made up his mind. He dived in beside

Westerly. 'Get the hell out of here!' he snapped.

He had to get away. As long as he remained free and unsuspected he still had a chance to reach the girl first. He pushed the gun into his pocket and removed his gloves. His hands were sweating and a nervous tic pulsed in his throat.

'Lucky we got false number plates,' Westerly grunted, swinging the wheel. 'They didn't get a clear look, so we're safe enough.'

Damn Gillespie, Dodd thought bitterly. Damn him to hell — the blasted blackmailer! He hoped he was suffering plenty, wherever he was. He brooded on his house and neglected motor business, Janet and the boy . . . all risked because a lush had to go and try to put the black on him. But he'd had to kill Gillespie. What else could he have done? Paid him, and gone on paying him for the rest of his life? Impossible. Gillespie's demands would have become ever more and more insupportable. And, as long as Gillespie lived, there'd always been the overhanging threat of prison . . . he shivered suddenly. A worse threat loomed over him now: a murder conviction.

He rubbed a sweating hand over his face.

And what about Arnie Bendix, the Ape? Was he safe? Arnie had certainly fouled things up badly when he'd burst into the Dean woman's flat. Maybe he ought to fix him, too . . . That television announcement had really put the pressure on. He had to shut Miss Doll Winters's mouth for her, or he was done for. His shoulders sagged. He felt old, and beaten.

Westerly drove fast, heading south to get across the river before the police closed their net. Both men knew that there would be a cordon round this area that night.

'Hell!' Gerald Dodd said aloud. 'Could I use a drink!'

And he wondered — *where was she now . . . ?*

★ ★ ★

Headlamps cutting a broad swathe of light through the darkness, Simon Brand pushed his MG sports car along at high speed. With Deputy Commander Walford beside him, he was on his way to a mews just off the Chelsea Embankment.

It had taken time to find Harry Hodges. It had taken even longer to sweat the truth out of him. But where the police were hampered by regulations, Brand was not. And Walford had left the two of them alone. So Hodges had talked . . .

That Hodges, Brand thought grimly, was one boy who would be up to his neck in trouble before he was very much older. Hodges had all the earmarks of a budding criminal.

Brand was angry about the delay — the killer had had nearly nine hours to find the Winters girl. Hodges had spilled all he knew to a man with odd-coloured eyes and tattooed hands.

That information had already been passed to Brand's young associate, combing the districts south of the river, and Brand wondered briefly how Nick was making out. It would help if his partner found a lead to the unknown's identity. They could close in more effectively that way — find the killer and take the pressure off the girl.

First things first, he decided. Nick hadn't come up with anything so far. Neither had there been any news from the office, nor from Marla Dean. And Walford knew all about the odd woman who called herself Miss Margaret . . .

The grey-haired, military-looking Scotland Yard man was speaking now as the sports car hurtled towards a rendezvous in Chelsea. 'We know her all right — we've had trouble with her before. She belongs to a peculiar group. They call themselves the Physologists, and some strange ideas of fun they have, too.'

He grimaced.

'It's all right between themselves, I suppose. Live and let live I say — until a complaint's made. But they don't always keep things in the family. That's when we're called in.'

Brand nodded absently, taking his foot off the accelerator as he threaded through traffic. Maybe the girl was safe. Even a group of cranks would not stand by and see murder done . . . but he wanted to get there fast. The faster the better. Time was definitely not on his side.

He trod on the accelerator again, and the powerful car leapt forward. Since midday, the killer had known where to find the Winters girl. And the killer was known to have helpers now. The sad-faced man in the bowler hat, whom Doll Winters had described to the police at Tooting was being assisted by Arnie Bendix, known among his friends as The Ape, and by a man with odd-coloured eyes and tattooed hands.

'There could be more of them involved, Walford,' he said, speaking his thoughts aloud. 'A car-stealing gang will have ramifications. There could be a whole network watching the roads for the Winters girl . . . and the Ape wouldn't be an easy man to hide. They'll have tried to smuggle him out of London.'

'We're working on it,' Walford said.

Simon Brand was not happy. The Winters girl had come to him and so far he hadn't been able to help. She was in danger — perhaps even dead, at this moment. Ruthlessly, he thrust the thought from him and concentrated on his driving.

There were lines of tiredness etched into his face. He had slept little since returning to London — and he would not rest until he knew that Miss Winters was safe. This was something personal, and he'd see it through. His jaw set determinedly as he swung into Chelsea Manor Street.

He saw the crowd, and braked smoothly. Eddies of smoke billowed from the mews, and he sniffed the air: burning oil. And then he heard gunshots . . .

'Drop me here,' Walford rapped. 'I recognize some of this lot.'

Brand halted long enough for Walford to duck out and slam the car door behind him. Then he threaded a way between fantastically dressed men and women and picked up speed.

He heard no more shooting, and saw no one. But his alert ears picked up the sound of a car engine fading in the distance as Walford's whistle shrilled out.

Brand cruised around, eyes hunting the shadows, listening for the slightest sound. Nothing. With a heavy heart, he circled once more, then headed back for Manor Street . . . it seemed they had arrived too late.

He parked the car and found Walford questioning a heavily made-up woman. 'I've got a good mind to book the lot of you!' Walford was declaring angrily. 'If anything happens to that girl, you'll be in trouble!'

'Doll Winters — ?' Brand put in quickly.

'She was here — but she's not now,' Walford flung back, and returned his attention to Miss Margaret. 'Come on, now! Speak up! Which way did she go?'

Miss Margaret pointed with a jewelled hand. 'She ran away . . . ran away from me. Base ingratitude, inspector! Really, if she came back to me now and begged to be taken in, I should refuse — '

Brand interrupted. 'Can you describe the gunman? I suppose you saw him?'

Miss Margaret stared at him; sniffed. 'A common man. He wore a bowler hat

— and such a long, sad face, too.'

'But he didn't hit the girl?'

'Hardly. She was running too fast for him.'

Walford said: 'From what I can make out, he faked a fire to get Miss Winters out of the house, and then missed her. These freaks made her dress up in a gym tunic, and she pulled on a large overcoat to cover herself — that probably saved her life.'

'Freaks!' Miss Margaret exclaimed. 'Well, really — !'

Walford said: 'I'll get a cordon thrown round the area. Brand. I don't think we'll catch the man we want, but we ought to find the girl. She can't be far away.' He turned to Miss Margaret again. 'Did Miss Winters have any money with her?'

'Certainly not! I don't believe in giving children pocket money. They have no sense of values these days.'

'So she's alone, without money, and wearing a dark overcoat over a school-girl's gym tunic,' Brand mused. 'She shouldn't be too hard to trace ... and we've got to find her first, Len. We've got to! His face was strained; his voice harsh. Doll Winters was too easily identifiable. She was a target.

'I'll phone and get the net set up,' Walford assured him.

Brand stared round at men in fancy dress, women with raddled, painted faces, others wearing grotesque masks. He felt nothing for them. He hardly saw them. His whole concentration was centred on one burning question:

Where was Doll Winters?

★　★　★

In medieval times, the Church was always a sanctuary. Here, fugitives were secure both from violence and the law. It was the last refuge of the hunted. So, perhaps, there was a certain rightness in the present case . . .

Doll Winters found a welcome peace of mind in that old English church: a renewal of the peace she had once found in Saint Cuthbert's.

Her nightmare passed. She could forget Miss Margaret and Professor McIntyre and the fire, and the shooting. The fire, she realized, had been intentionally started: a trick to get her out of the house.

And she shivered suddenly . . . the man in the bowler hat had almost got her there. It had been a close thing; the first time anyone had ever fired at her with a gun. She hadn't liked it at all, and had no desire to repeat the experience.

Once she remembered — and it seemed a long time ago — she had wished that something exciting might happen to her. She had been achingly emptily lonely, and had longed for something to brighten her life. Now she regretted that wish. She wanted only to get back to normality. But wishing was not going to stop a faller.

She had to get away. Anywhere. Out of London, she decided, that was the answer. Get out of London, where the killer would never find her again.

The empty church was quiet and lent her some of its remote calm. Fear had left her, to be replaced by a nagging worry. How was she to get out of London? She had no money, and there was no one she could turn to for help. She had gone to the police . . . and they had turned her away. That was the trouble. Right from the start, no one had believed her.

For a moment, she felt tempted to break open the collection box just inside the door of the church — but was immediately ashamed of the impulse. She couldn't do that. But she still had to get out of London somehow.

Doll had only a vague idea of geography beyond the limits of Tooting Bec. But she knew that it cost money to travel. And she needed clothes too. Besides being ridiculous garb for a young woman of eighteen the gym tunic was sparse enough to leave her shivering with cold in that draughty, unheated place. At least she could be grateful for the warmth afforded by the overcoat.

She began to wonder how much time had passed. She had heard two cars go by. Surely the coast must be clear by now, she thought, looking up at a text hanging on the wall: PUT THY TRUST IN THE LORD.

Doll Winters was not a deeply religious person. Neither, unlike her mother, did she ever lay claim to being one. But, already, she was feeling better.

Perhaps He would protect her. Perhaps He had been with her all the time . . . it was a nice thought to hold on to.

But now it was time to move on.

Standing beneath the dark stained glass windows, she looked up at the figure on the cross above the altar. She drew strength from it, knowing that somehow she was no longer alone in her trouble.

She left the church, walking warily in the shadows. She had no sense of direction and no idea where she was until she came to a brightly-lit main road. A wall plate read: FULHAM ROAD — but that didn't mean much to her, either.

Farther down the road, at the corner of Redcliffe Gardens, were traffic lights set at red. A heavy lorry rolled past and drew up at the lights. Doll quickened her step. It looked the sort of lorry that might be travelling through the night, out of London . . .

Perhaps if she spoke to the driver

. . . And then she remembered. Harry Hodges. She didn't want that kind of trouble again. It seemed to Doll that, in this cruel world, everyone wanted payment of some sort for the slightest favour.

There was a tarpaulin drawn over the lorry's cargo. Doll darted a quick look round to ensure that she was unobserved then stepped into the road behind the lorry, out of view of the driver's rear mirror. She swung herself up and burrowed deep under the tarpaulin. She curled up among a load of cardboard boxes.

The lorry moved off, heading west out of London, as the lights changed.

But the fear of death still lay heavy in Doll Winters's heart.

10

A Breath Of Country Air

Simon Brand's young partner, Nick Chandler, was not making much progress. Working in liaison with the Tooting police, he had viewed the suspected murder scene, and questioned Doll Winters's ex-landlady and her mother. He had visited the factory of Levinson Structural Steel Fabrications Limited, where Doll had worked. And he still had no lead to a long, sad-faced man who was partial to wearing a bowler hat.

But he was getting a picture of Doll Winters herself. That was something. The girl was beginning to come alive for him . . .

He remembered her mother, standing outside a mean terraced cottage and saying at him in a shrill voice: 'I don't want to know! If she's in trouble, I'm not surprised! Let her get herself out of it!

134

I'm a respectable woman!'

The door had slammed in his face.

He remembered a young constable on the beat saying: 'Doll's highly imaginative, y'know . . . '

The jackal-eyed factory manageress. 'Doll? A good worker — when she wasn't daydreaming. Always got her head stuck into some sloppy magazine. She wasn't one to make friends easily — a rather lonely girl, I'd say.'

And Miss Legge, her landlady, head on one side, henna-red hair shining dully in the light from the window, pecking the words out. 'A nice girl. Very clean. Easy to get on with. I liked her a lot. Very young, of course. Only eighteen . . . ' A pause. Then, more slowly, 'A lonely child . . . '

A girl at the factory. 'She was dead slow! Never dated boys — she seemed scared of 'em. Not like me at all!' Bold eyes ogled Brand's tough, blond young partner. 'I'm not doing anything tonight, either, just as it happens . . . '

Nick was. And he was more worried than ever about Doll Winters. The more he learned about her, the more worried he became. He wanted her to be all right. He had built up a picture of a rather nice girl: a daydreamer, certainly, but only because the life she was living was totally uninspired. A rather lonely girl, but not because she wasn't attractive in her way, just because she was fastidious. And what would she do now with a killer after her, and no friends . . . ?

He questioned shop assistants along the High Street. One, a green-eyed leggy redhead, told him: 'Sure, I know Doll. Used to come in here for chocolate sometimes. I saw a man following her — stocky-like, with a tattoo mark on the back of his hand.'

Nick phoned the office and learned from Miss Rington that Brand was also interested in a man with tattooed hands. He began to feel that he was getting somewhere at long last.

Casting his net over a steadily widening area of South London, he checked garages that looked as though they might be a hideaway for stolen cars. He asked questions and he kept his eyes open. For once, a routine inquiry held a sense of urgency for him . . . a lone girl's life was threatened as she was tailed by an implacable killer.

And, eventually, he arrived in Norbury.

★   ★   ★

Autumn sunlight turned fallen leaves into a rich, golden-brown carpet. Birdsong floated on air at once clean and crisp. And the tree trunk of an old elm splintered under the edge of a double-bladed axe, the chips flying as the big, powerful man split the wood and piled the logs neatly.

Arnie Bendix, more usually called the Ape, late of Islington, was feeling happy. He liked fresh air and exercise. It reminded him of his training days in the long-ago when he had been a professional wrestler.

He swung the axe with practised ease, a huge-muscled man with a stupid, homely face, thinking how nice it was to be away from the smoke and grime of London, and staying at a small farm deep in the country for a few days.

He had been driven down by a uniformed chauffeur, everything arranged for him. He had money in his pocket, more money than he'd seen in a very long time. Why shouldn't he be happy?

Arnie the Ape was slow on the uptake, but he knew a man had to keep fit. He swung his axe with relish and carefully piled the logs high for the winter store. No one bothered him here. His comic papers were provided, and he neither drank nor smoked.

Women had a tendency to look at him and run; a sad fact. But the one at the farm was pleasant enough to him. Mr. Dodd was a real pal fixing this for him . . .

Arnie Bendix knew that he wasn't bright, and only got the jobs requiring muscle. Others provided the brainpower, and he was quite happy about that, too. In his experience, cleverness did not seem to make people any nicer.

He felt guilty about that girl, though. She had seemed a nice kid, but she'd been scared and had bolted like a rabbit. And, really, he wouldn't have hurt her

— but Mr. Dodd wanted her out in the open for some reason of his own. Forget it, he told himself, swinging the axe again.

A woman's voice called from the house: 'Your coffee's ready, Mr. Bendix.'

That was nice, too, he thought. Few people called him 'Mister' or ever used his surname. Few? None at all! Not that he resented being called an ape. The mirror confirmed the unhappy fact of his appearance every morning as he shaved. But it was still nice to be called 'Mr. Bendix'. And by a woman, too . . . a young one . . . a widow.

'Coming,' he said, and laid down his axe with some care. He had a respect for tools.

He shambled back to the farmhouse, watching woodsmoke coil lazily up from a red brick chimney. The farm was screened by trees, isolated, well away from any main road. He hardly saw anyone, but that didn't bother him either. Mr. Dodd had promised him a good job when he returned to London, Don Westerly said.

He crossed a tiled floor, sat easily in a

big chair. 'Have my comics come?' he asked.

'Yes, Mr. Bendix — they're here.' Smiling, the neat, red-lipped woman passed them across to him. She had a newspaper, he noticed, the *Daily Post*. And glaring headlines caught his eye:

HAVE YOU SEEN THIS GIRL?

He had! There was a picture splashed across the front page. A picture of the girl he had scared out of the flat in Lowndes Square. He said politely, 'Do you mind if I have a look at that?'

The young widow seemed surprised. Not surprised that he could read, but surprised that he should be interested in a newspaper. He had never shown any interest in one before. 'Of course not, Mr. Bendix,' she said briskly, and passed the paper to him.

Arnie the Ape read carefully, word by word, his lips moving slowly. He read all the sensational facts set down in cold print.

'*This girl is in danger of losing her life!* Doll Winters, from Tooting Bec — '

Tooting, Arnie reflected, was a long

way from Lowndes Square, Knights-bridge. It couldn't be the same girl after all . . .

' — disappeared from Lowndes Square . . . sole witness to murder . . . a killer out to silence her. If you see this girl, report to the nearest police station immediately!'

There followed a description.

It *was* the same girl. This knowledge penetrated slowly. But Mr. Dodd wouldn't kill anyone, Arnie decided. Lift a few cars, sure. There was nothing wrong in that . . . but murder? Not Mr. Gerald Dodd. Arnie Bendix had a problem. An uneasiness descended upon him as he read: 'The dead man, Sean Gillespie . . . ' He knew Gillespie vaguely. It could be . . . Mr. Dodd must have gone daft, killing Gillespie.

'Newspaper talk,' he said out loud. 'You can't believe half of what you read in the papers. Just lies! They make it all up.'

He dismissed the story from his mind. Almost. There was still a tiny nagging doubt, and Arnie Bendix was a harmless, amiable creature who wouldn't want to see a pretty young girl get hurt.

Perhaps he ought to go to the police. Perhaps he ought to see Mr. Dodd first though, and explain . . . something told him that would be the wrong thing to do, though, if Mr. Dodd were really set on killing somebody.

'Your coffee's getting cold, Mr. Bendix,' the young widow said mystified by the expressions struggling across his battered face.

'Coffee . . . yes, thank you.' He smiled at the woman. She was nice he thought. So considerate.

He gulped down the coffee, not liking the idea of squealing on anyone. Squealers were not popular. Arnie the Ape brooded on this He was still thinking about what he might do when he stepped outside and took up his axe again.

A man thought more clearly when he was working.

★ ★ ★

'Well . . . ?' Janet Dodd demanded, facing her husband across their big, contemporary living room at Norbury. 'Well . . . ?

142

Suppose you give me a few answers. I'm tired of being left in the dark. Something's going on, and I want to know what.'

Gerald Dodd lifted a haggard face from the front page of the *Daily Post*. He, too, had been reading the lead story. 'Well, what? There's nothing going on, Janet. Nothing.'

'So you look like a man who's just lost his money on the stock market. Gerald, it's not that, is it?' Janet had been reading how the New York crash had affected the London market.

'No, it's not that,' he answered wearily.

'But you're never in the house these days, nor at the garage. Always chasing off somewhere. Is it another woman?' She was calm now. 'I've a right to know, Gerald.'

Dodd groaned silently. As if he hadn't enough on his mind! 'No, it's not another woman . . . I wish it were! Perhaps I'd get some peace from her. Now shut up!' He had heartburn again, unwrapped a lozenge and placed it on his tongue. 'I've told you before,' he grumbled. 'I like my steak well-cooked.'

'Then cook it yourself — or get your fancy woman to do it!' She was near to tears. 'And what about Paul? I'm keeping him, whatever you decide.'

'Janet,' Dodd said, struggling to control his voice, 'for the last time — there is no other woman. Forget that stuff! I've got business worries, that's all. I'll straighten out — given time.'

He returned his attention to the newspaper. It could only be a question of time before someone spotted the girl and told the police — but why hadn't she been seen already? In that gym tunic, much too small for her, she would stick out like a sore thumb when she took her coat off . . . and she had to take it off sometime, or she'd look equally odd. The boys hadn't seen her, either. She must have skipped out of town somehow. A lorry driver . . . ? That was something to follow up.

Janet said: 'Can I do anything to help? I'll do anything, Gerald. Just tell me what sort of trouble you're in.'

'Oh, shut up, Janet,' he grunted, and

poured himself a drink.

Janet flushed.

She had a new hairstyle, and he hadn't even noticed. 'It's not like you to drink in the daytime,' she said. 'I know there's something wrong — terribly wrong.'

Gerald Dodd suddenly crushed the newspaper into a ball and hurled it across the room. 'Damn it, Janet, lay off!' he shouted, and then instantly regretted the outburst. He couldn't afford to quarrel with her, now. 'Listen, if anyone comes round asking questions, I haven't been out. Got that? *I haven't been out.*'

He rubbed a hand over his jaw. He ought to shave and show himself at the garage. He must keep up appearances . . . it had been a sweat getting back last night, changing the plates. A near thing, with Brand and the cops. His hand shook as he thought about it.

Now the cops knew that Gillespie had been murdered. No doubt they believed the girl's story. But only she could testify against him — and he'd find her soon and shut her mouth. He had to. But where in hell was she?

145

'Ger — '

Gerald Dodd rose and put his arm around his wife. 'Forget it, Janet. It'll work out.' He prayed that it would, because he stood to lose everything now. Already he could feel the net dragging tighter about him.

Standing there, in his comfortable home with his arm round his wife, he shivered as though with the ague.

★   ★   ★

The lorry carrying Doll Winters sped through the night, travelling fast. It stopped once, near Hammersmith flyover, as police flagged it down and a constable said: 'We're looking for a girl of eighteen wearing a dark coat and a gym tunic. Anyone like that asked you for a lift tonight?'

'Nah!' The driver spat. 'Anyway, I wouldn't give no lift to a bird. Too risky.'

He drove on.

Deep under the tarpaulin, in a dark green world, Doll Winters was asleep and dreaming. Subconsciously, she heard the brief exchange, and once again she was a gun moll on the run.

' . . . Step on the gas, Duke! The cops are stopping all cars, and I've got to beat this rap . . . '

She slept through Chiswick and Brentford, cramped among the boxes stacked all around her. But finally, the bouncing and swaying motion of the lorry bruised her arms and legs and jolted her awake, and back to her present predicament.

She remembered another ride: a time she had hitched a lift to the south coast. She had walked out over Brighton pier and seen the sea for the first time in her life. She had been alone then, too. She couldn't swim, but it had been nice to look at the sea, and something to think about for weeks afterwards.

The lorry roared on, headlamps slicing a bright runway through the darkness. Presently, it swerved and began to climb a hill. Finally it stopped outside yard gates where harsh electric arcs burned. Men's voices echoed, and the driver climbed down, lit a cigarette, grumbling: 'Ruddy nightwork — I've had enough of it. Some of these office boys want to have a go . . . '

It was the end of the journey.

Doll sneaked out from under cover and cautiously lowered herself to the ground. A man turned and saw her. He bawled: 'Hi, you there — stop!'

Doll had heard that kind of voice before. She knew the last thing you did was stop — if you had any sense. She took to her heels and ran . . .

A dark road stretched before her, long and empty, and she ran between shadowy trees and silent houses, not knowing where she was, and not caring. She heard running feet behind her and another shout.

'Stop!'

The road seemed to peter out in a countrified lane with grass banks and telegraph poles. Ahead loomed a hump-backed bridge. Again she thought she heard running footsteps behind her. It might have been the shadow of a tree swaying in the night wind. It might have been the shadow of a man . . .

Doll didn't hesitate. She swung herself over the low wall, hung a moment, then dropped. It was a long drop.

The icy water closed over her head.

11

On The Grand

Fred Baron was suffering. The lower half of his jaw felt stiff and swollen as a back tooth alternately throbbed and stabbed. He tossed and turned under the blankets in sleepless agony; finally, unable to contain the pain any longer, he flung back the bedclothes and crawled out of the bunk.

He had forgotten just where he was, and, in the dark, hit his head on the low ceiling. 'Blast!' He fumbled for matches and lit a swinging oil lamp at his third attempt. It smoked badly and set him coughing. Tea, he thought, make a pot of tea — maybe that would deaden his awful nagging toothache.

He felt exhausted, worn out by his long battle for sleep against the decayed molar that plagued him. He should have had it out long before, he told himself, and winced at a mental image of a glittering array of probes and steel pincers. Fred Baron had an abiding horror of dentists. Sadists, he called them.

He fiddled with the calor gas stove and got it burning. He filled a kettle and set it over the flame. It seemed to take ages to boil, and he paced restlessly up and down the tiny cabin.

A holiday spent cruising the canals ... what a farce! Everything had gone wrong. His mate, Horace, had been keen on the idea — till a girl changed his mind for him. The trip was fixed, the boat paid for, and then Harold had said: 'Sorry, Fred, but Vi and me, we're going away to Clacton together.'

Fred Baron had only grunted. He was going cruising anyway. But handling a boat single-handed, he found, wasn't much fun. And taking the small cabin-cruiser *Phoebe* through a long series of locks had been desperately hard work — Fred's hands were raw and blistered from the effort. And now — toothache!

He picked up a luridly-covered paper-back and started to read a chapter while he waited for the kettle to boil . . .

He'd left Brentford, opposite Kew Gardens, that morning, fumbling his first lock badly. The Grand Union Canal meandered through Hanwell and Southall and West Drayton; and he had moored for the first night of his holiday near Cowley. He was fed up and he felt like chucking the whole thing and returning home. A holiday was no fun on one's own.

The kettle boiled, and he spooned tea into the pot. Then he remembered that he had no fresh milk. And he daren't risk sugar with raging toothache. Hell! Tea without milk or sugar — it was like a bad dream.

He went on reading the paperback while he waited for the tea to draw. What a situation, he thought . . . a beautiful blonde left with her ex-lover's corpse on her hands, and trying to get rid of it.

That was when he heard something fall into the canal with a loud splash . . .

★   ★   ★

The canals of England project from the Midlands like the spokes from the hub of a wheel, reaching across the length and breadth of the country. Most of them were built during the Industrial Revolution, in the eighteenth century, when packhorse trains travelling overland could not cope with the large supplies of fuel and raw materials demanded by an ever-growing number of factories.

The roads then were often little more than cart tracks, inches deep in mud. Rivers had a habit of not running where they were, required. And the internal combustion and steam engine had not grown up. So the canals came into their own as an important means of transport.

The man-made waterways had spread rapidly. Heavy boats carried coal and stone and agricultural produce. Smaller boats handled general merchandise and parcels, while fast packets ran a regular passenger service.

These boats were long and narrow, brightly painted, and drawn by horses — except where the engineer had burrowed a tunnel through a hillside.

Here, power was supplied by 'legging'. Special boards like outriggers were laid across the forepart of the boat, and the boatmen lay on their backs on these projecting wings, thrusting with their feet against the walls of the tunnel.

As time passed, the monotonous throb of diesel engines replaced the steady clip-clopping of horses; but life on the cuts remained much the same. The boatman took his wife with him. Their children remained on the boat, and eventually married children from other boats. A tight little community grew up, gypsies of the waterways, living a nomadic life.

The canal boatmen evolved their own technique of navigation; speed meant money to them, for they were paid by the trip. To work a seventy foot long boat through a series of locks at speed required meticulous handling and co-operation on the part of the entire family. And the constant attention that must be paid to steering along a narrow cut is wearisome work.

Then the railways came, and the canal

era passed. The canals gradually dropped into disuse. Only a few boats remained to ply the main arteries of the system. Weed-choked, rubble-filled, the man-made waterways became overgrown and hidden; and some weekend fisherman, stumbling across one in the wilds of the countryside, might never guess it was not a natural stream.

A new era opened up for the canals when teenagers found they could use small cabin cruisers on them. It was the ideal way for youngsters seeking to get away from the dirt and the noise of towns to rediscover the peace and quiet of the English scene. Weekends extended to a fortnight's holiday cruising the canals . . . pleasure cruising in every sense of the word, remote and isolated from everyday life.

It gave them a sense of adventure, of getting away from the car-jammed roads; gave them a feeling of solitude and silence; a chance to pioneer and open up the old waterways.

They found a quiet beauty as they cruised slowly through the green heart of old England, following the cuts through woodland and meadow, passing beneath a range of hills or crossing a valley via aqueduct. It was — *sanctuary*.

★　★　★

Doll Winters screamed as she went under, but no sound came out because her mouth was filled with dirty, choking canal water. She spluttered and struggled wildly as panic surged through her. So this was what it was like to die . . . but no pictures of her past life flashed across the screen of her mind. Doll was disappointed. She felt cheated. The flashes-of-past-life thing always happened in the best books and pictures . . .

She surfaced, spitting water, arms flapping, and managed to struggle out of her heavy coat. She saw a bulky shadow looming above her. A boat!

'Help!' she called, fighting to keep afloat. 'Help! I can't swim!'

She glimpsed movement on deck and heard a voice answer. 'Hold on!' The dark figure was fumbling with something. A wooden pole with a curved metal hook at the end of it was suddenly thrust at her. Doll grasped it, peering upwards fearfully in the night gloom. She saw a square, startled face topped by a mass of unruly chestnut hair; a rugged male body with a coat worn over pyjamas.

Then he was hauling her inboard and they stood facing each other. Doll, shivering in a dripping-wet gym tunic too small for her and shrinking rapidly. He, staring at her with bulging, incredulous eyes.

'Thanks,' Doll gasped, and made a face. 'I never knew water could taste so bad!'

'You'd better come into the cabin,' Fred Baron said. 'I can give you a hot drink.'

Doll ducked through a low opening. It was warm in the cabin with a stove burning and the oil lamp swinging, a bunk on either side of a folding table. 'Drink that down,' he said, pointing at the steaming cup of tea, and pulled a spare army-surplus blanket off one of the bunks. 'Here, you'd better get out of those wet clothes.'

Doll set down the cup and faced him squarely. 'Not in front of you,' she said firmly. It seemed to her she'd been through all this before.

'Oh . . . well . . . ah . . . I'll go on deck. Don't be too long, though. My name's Fred Baron, by the way.'

'Mine's Doll Winters.'

Fred stepped out of the cabin and Doll stripped and rubbed herself dry. She forgot to draw the curtains across the window, but Fred — after a quick peek — turned his back. She seemed a nice girl, he thought, and began to wonder about her. What on earth had made her jump into the canal in the middle of the night? And she seemed a big girl to be wearing a gymslip.

Doll, meanwhile, had hung her wet clothes round the stove and wrapped herself in a blanket. 'You can come back in now,' she called.

Fred Baron obeyed and poured tea. He'd forgotten about his aching tooth in the excitement — until the hot tea got at it. Then his face screwed up in an expression of agony.

'Toothache,' he mumbled, massaging his jaw.

'I *am* sorry,' Doll said.

They sat facing each other, on opposite bunks across the table, drinking tea, wondering what happened next. 'You can stay here for a while if you want,' Fred Baron said. 'I'm on holiday. Just going to cruise up the canal a bit.'

'Canal?' Doll looked blank.

Fred explained: 'The Grand Union. It goes up north. My pal let me down, and I'm stuck for crew — '

A canal that headed away out of London, Doll thought. It sounded like the perfect escape route. She'd never even heard of it before and, very likely, the sad-faced killer in the bowler hat hadn't heard of it either. This seemed like the answer to her problem. No one would think of looking on a canal for her.

She glanced quickly, but carefully at Fred Baron. Alone with a young man on a boat . . . but he looked a decent sort, not like that Harry from the *Torero*. It was a chance she'd have to take, Doll decided

'I'm hungry,' she said suddenly. 'You got anything to eat on this boat — er — Fred?'

Fred Baron looked startled for the second time that night. He just wasn't used to girls dropping in for a midnight snack. 'I guess so,' he admitted, and thought about it. 'We can have a fry-up.'

He greased the pan while Doll made more tea, and she told him her problem as they ate sausages and bacon and eggs and fried bread. Fred listened with growing wonder, not quite knowing how much to believe. It just didn't seem possible. She was really extraordinary, this girl, but pretty . . .

He took a quick look at her trim figure huddled under the rough blanket and thought his holiday had taken a turn for the better. With this girl, Doll, aboard, the coming cruise could be fun.

'I'll take you up the canal,' he said. 'You'll be safe enough with me.'

Doll Winters looked hard at him. 'All right,' she agreed. 'But no funny business, mind.'

'No funny business,' Fred Baron said gravely. He had forgotten his toothache now.

★ ★ ★

'I don't like it,' Don Westerly growled. 'That bird must be somewhere. Someone should have spotted her by now.'

Gerald Dodd scowled at his foreman. He didn't want to be reminded of his damoclean sword. They sat together, Westerly smoking, in Dodd's private office at the back of the garage. Beyond the glass of the windows, mechanics were busy disguising stolen cars . . .

'We'll hear soon enough,' he answered.

'We'd better,' Westerly said darkly. 'I don't like to think what Simon Brand might be doing. If he gets on to us here, were in dead trouble.'

'We're in trouble anyway,' Dodd reflected sourly. He felt desperate. It was *him* facing a murder charge.

Westerly stubbed out his cigarette butt and picked up a racing paper. 'That Bob,' he said idly, 'he's real artistic with a spray-gun — '

The phone pealed and Dodd scooped it up, one-handed. 'Gerald Dodd.' He listened, expression changing. 'Found her,' he mouthed sideways at Westerly. 'Yes, yes . . . I've got that . . . right, Uxbridge will be fine . . . good . . . yes, don't worry, you'll be well paid!'

He replaced the receiver and stood up.

'Get changed, Don. We're taking to the water. Try to look like someone on holiday. You know, flannels, open-neck shirt, rope-soled shoes. We're hiring a boat at Uxbridge. The Winters girl is sailing up the Grand Union Canal.'

Westerly whistled soundlessly. 'Is she, indeed! That bird certainly gets around. This couldn't be better, eh . . . ? Pretty lonely on a canal, and lots of accidents happen on boats. It wouldn't surprise me if she drowned . . . you know that? I don't suppose she can swim.'

'That's certainly a thought,' Dodd agreed, gloating.

Another accident . . . with no witness

around this time.

'Let's get moving,' he said. 'We're going to get that skirt this time, and shut her mouth for keeps!'

12

Pursuit

Sunlight flashed on the chromium and scarlet façade of a garage in London Road, Norbury. High above, a sign read: G. DODD — CAR MART. As Nick Chandler, Brand's partner, swung his Jaguar into the corner lot and parked in front of the petrol pumps, he saw a black saloon draw away . . .

He thought nothing of it at that moment.

'Fill her up,' he told the pump attendant, and looked about him with casual interest. The place sprawled over quite a large area, and there were workshops farther back. G. Dodd Esquire dealt in second-hand cars — a good cover. It could be, Nick thought, and got out.

The pump attendant looked at him quickly.

'Had a long ride,' Nick said with a smile, and stretched. He strolled about, unobtrusively studying the layout. He stuck a cigarette in his mouth, but refrained from lighting it.

This could be it, he decided, the place he was looking for. It was by far the most likely place he'd yet come across . . . how many garages he'd conned so far he had no idea. Twenty . . . ? Thirty . . . ? He'd really lost count. But still there was a nagging sense of urgency in him. He remembered little Doll Winters with a killer after her . . . yes, this garage would bear investigating more thoroughly, and as soon as possible.

'I'm having some kind of intermittent trouble with my flashers,' he said, returning to the Jaguar. 'Just check them over, will you? I'll be back in about an hour.'

'Very good, sir.'

The attendant hardly noticed as Nick walked away. Round the corner he found a narrow lane bordering the garage yard. A high wall, topped by barbed wire, circled it. There was a door; locked.

Nick took a swift look round to ensure that he was unobserved, and then got to work on the lock. His skeleton key turned the tumblers and he opened the door and slid inside, closing the door gently behind him. This rear entrance led directly to the workshops.

The sound of a compressor attracted him and he moved swiftly to a window of the spray-shop and looked in.

An overalled mechanic was doing a paint-job on what looked to be a brand-new car.

Nick's eyes narrowed.

Another man was bolting on fresh number plates . . .

Interest quickened in Nick as he watched. He had the feeling that he was finally on the verge of a breakthrough. Mr. G. Dodd's Car Mart needed looking into. It was time to start asking some pertinent questions . . .

The tingling down his spine came a fraction of a second too late.

He wheeled around, and there was a man behind him swinging a heavy spanner. Nick threw up an arm in an attempt to ward off the vicious blow, but didn't entirely succeed. The blow fell, and he'd saved his skull, but a shockwave of pain leapt all the way along the length of the arm to his shoulder.

He staggered; recovered; got his back to the wall as the man with the spanner swung at him again and distantly someone shouted: 'Hey, Bob! Look there! Snooper!'

Another man came running.

Nick's right arm was numb. It was useless. He tried to defend himself with his left. The two men came at him together.

One dived for his ankles as the man with the spanner again swung at his head. All three of them went down in a heap.

Nick kicked one man in the face, used a knee on the other and managed to break free. He rolled over, scrambled on to his feet, and started to run. He'd learned all he needed to know. Honest mechanics didn't attack a stranger on sight. These men were up to something crooked. He could guess what it was. And he had to get away to pass the word to Simon Brand.

But Nick had reckoned without a patch of oil. His feet hit it, and skidded away from beneath him. He went down again and the two garage-hands had him. The spanner slammed down across his skull and consciousness reeled.

'Get him out of sight,' he heard one rasp to the other. 'I dunno what the boss is going to say, but we can't let this yobbo loose to shoot off his mouth.'

Nick had only a confused impression of what happened next.

He felt himself dragged across concrete. Thin cord bit into his wrists and ankles. A gag half-choked him. He was rolled to the edge of an inspection pit, and pushed over.

For a very brief instant of time, he struggled ineffectually as he fell. Then there was a moment of impact, and there was pain.

Nick Chandler's last, enduring impression was of a powerful smell of oil.

★ ★ ★

The good ship *Phoebe* glided effortlessly between meadows and fields and hedges under a clear blue sky. To Doll Winters, clad in a pair of Fred Baron's slacks and a sweater, it was a glimpse of another world. The canal — disrespectfully called 'the cut' by the boatmen — reached north through tranquil countryside, remote from the hustle and clamour of frenetic city life.

It was late for the holiday season and there was little traffic; and she stared, fascinated, at her first narrow boat as it approached. Seventy feet long yet only seven feet wide, the wooden canal boat was decorated with roses and castles painted in gaudy reds and yellows and blues. A thin black funnel jutted from the cabin aft, and a boatman's wife leaned nonchalantly against the massive tiller.

Doll felt envious. It would be wonderful to be a boatman's wife, she decided, and spend the rest of her life in quiet serenity. She darted a quick look at Fred Baron standing at the wheel of the motorboat, a stubby pipe clenched in his mouth, and her dream expanded . . . Now she was aboard a luxury yacht cruising the ocean, and Fred was a star of the silver screen carrying her off on their honeymoon.

She felt relaxed for the first time in days. No more trouble, she thought happily. No one was going to find her now. And nothing had happened in the night except that she had learned that Fred snored.

She gazed dreamily at reflections in the water. Trees, a church steeple, cows, a magpie on a branch. Blackberries grew beside the towpath and white clouds drifted high in. the sky. She glimpsed the red roofs of a village far in the distance.

They passed under a stone bridge and emerged into woodland, screened from the rest of the world. 'It's beautiful,' Doll sighed wistfully. 'I wish we could go on and on and on for ever!'

Fred Baron pulled at the pipe in his mouth. 'Very pleasant — er — Doll,' he agreed. 'Makes a chap feel good to be alive. Better than being stuck in a factory all day.'

'You in a factory too? I was operating a capstan.'

'I'm a tool-maker by trade,' Fred Baron said. 'Not bad pay, and there's plenty of overtime.'

Doll thought rapidly. That sounded enough to marry on. 'You're not married?' she asked quickly.

'No. Never met Miss Right, I suppose — though I'm not saying I shan't be interested when she comes along.'

Doll's heart thumped pleasantly. She imagined what it would be like to wash Fred's shirts and darn his socks . . . they had the same background . . . he was her sort, all right. She dreamed again. It would only be a small house, but nice, and they'd start a family right away . . . true love, just like the magazines.

She sighed again. So far, Mr. Baron hadn't seemed romantically inclined. She shot another look at him. Well, she had a fortnight to prod him into proposing.

'Lock coming up, Doll,' Fred said. 'You take the wheel. Just keep her steady and ease off when I tell you. I'll work the lock. Okay?'

'Aye, aye, skipper!' she said cheerfully, throwing him a salute.

Fred stepped on to the bank, windlass in hand, and Doll was left in command of the *Phoebe*. She gazed fondly at him as he wound up the paddles.

Doll Winters felt good. The past, she thought, was behind her. She was enjoying life, almost for the first time . . . and planning a future. She had found her man. The danger was over. She felt safe now; secure in her newly-found happiness.

But Mr. Gerald Dodd had other ideas.

★ ★ ★

A black Rover Saloon swung into the boatyard at Uxbridge and two men climbed out, hefting weekend bags.

Gerald Dodd, in cream-coloured flannels and a blue jacket with brass buttons, looked a changed man. Doll would not have known him without his bowler hat. Don Westerly sported reddish-brown slacks and a roll-neck sweater. His

172

tattooed hands lent him an authentic nautical air.

They might have been a couple of city workers relaxing for a few days — there was nothing about them to suggest that their business was murder.

The man waiting for them touched his cap. His voice whined unpleasantly. 'I got her spotted, boss, soon as she dropped off that lorry. She's on a small cruiser, *Phoebe* they call it. And there's a bloke with her. They've gone north, up the canal — you'll pick 'em up with no trouble at all.'

Don Westerly leered. 'A bloke with her, you say? Some guys get all the luck!' He swung his head, sharing his leer with Gerald Dodd. 'Pity you didn't lay on a couple of pieces for us, boss, while you were about it.'

He remembered the Chinese girl at the *Strippery* in Soho. He wouldn't mind sharing a berth with her . . .

Todd said harshly: 'Pipe down, Don. This is strictly business.' His feelings felt constricted. Now that the showdown was fast approaching, he felt an aversion for what he had to do. Still, maybe the man with her could be got out of the way. Maybe it could be made to look like an accident. The gun in his pocket was a dead weight. He was sick of the whole sordid mess.

But he had to go through with it. He had to shut Doll Winters's mouth for good and all.

The three men walked across the yard, past the skeleton of a narrow boat under construction, where a smell of oak shavings hung in the air. Old tillers were stacked against one wall of a paint shed, and a sound of hammering came from the direction of the forge. They reached the canal side of the yard, where a variety of boats lay moored in the dock.

'Yours is the big cabin cruiser, boss. It's all ready for you. I seen to everythin'.'

'Some beer aboard?' Dodd grunted, passing over a wad of notes.

'Sure, boss — two crates. And a couple of bottles of whisky.'

Dodd scowled. He'd need a drink on this job. Janet had been suspicious when he'd packed his bag. Now she was sure he was going off with another woman. He wished he were . . .

He stepped aboard the cruiser, a four-berth boat with bow-fender, light-blue paintwork, and windlasses neatly stowed in the cockpit. He slung his bag inside the cabin. 'Let's get started,' he said tautly.

As Westerly cast off the mooring lines, he got the engine going and took the steering wheel. Westerly paddled inboard and dropped down into the cockpit as the cruiser slid smoothly out of the dock and headed north up the canal.

'Notice the name we got on the bows, boss?' Westerly asked. And Dodd had. 'Kinda appropriate, don't you think?' Westerly went on, and chuckled. The name of the boat was *The Hunter*.

'Sure is going to be one hell of a surprise for the Winters piece when we catch up with her!' Westerly said.

Gerald Dodd didn't answer. He concentrated on his steering. He didn't even want to think about what lay ahead.

Sure, he had to do it. He had to kill the girl, Winters. He had to silence her. It was her life or his. And that gave him no choice.

But he didn't want to think about it, just the same. Cold-blooded murder wasn't really his cup of tea.

13

A Spot Of Bad Luck

A large-scale map of London and the surrounding area covered one wall of the operations room at New Scotland Yard.

The map was studded with tiny, coloured flags.

The windows of the room were shut. Tobacco smoke hung like mist in the air. In the background, constantly, printers chattered away.

In front of the map, Deputy-Commander Walford breathed hard. His eyes were troubled. 'There's no sign of her. No sign at all,' he said. She's just disappeared into thin air.'

Simon Brand nodded thoughtfully, snapping his lighter to a fresh cigarette.

'It's ridiculous,' Walford went on in harassed tones. 'All our men have been alerted, the roads watched. A picture of the girl has been put out over all southern television networks, and has appeared in the newspapers. You'd think all that would result in something.'

He was exasperated.

'Dammit,' he growled, 'we've got this whole blasted area sewn up really tight, and have had ever since the girl scampered out of Miss Margaret's place. She can't have got out of London. And someone must have seen her. It just isn't possible that she could disappear without trace! She has no money — no friends. We know that she has no friends. So where in hell is she? Why hasn't she been spotted? It just isn't reasonable — unless — '

And there he paused briefly.

Then he said, very uneasily, 'Unless the killer's got to her.'

And his apprehension was naked and real.

But then Brand spoke — briskly. 'I don't think so, Len. Not yet. Remember, it's just as tough for him as it is for us. More so in fact.'

He brooded over the wall-map.

Obviously, somehow and somewhere,

Doll Winters must have broken through the net the police had thrown around Greater London. Walford didn't think that it could be done, but it must have been done. Somehow and somewhere, Doll Winters had got through the cordon. And not by road. On the roads, she'd have been picked up long before this.

Simon Brand had another problem on his mind. His associate, Nick Chandler, also seemed to have vanished. Brand's mouth moved grimly. Of course, Nick might be following a hot lead and be unable to telephone . . . but it was worrying, just the same. The fact that Nick was on the trail of a killer was enough to worry Brand.

With an effort, he put all thoughts of Nick out of his mind and concentrated on Doll Winters. 'She's slipped through the net,' he said slowly.

'Impossible,' Walford returned shortly.

He said: 'We've covered every road with checkpoints set in a pattern of concentric circles. She might have got through one — even two — if she were

179

hidden under the load on a back of a lorry, say, or something like that. But she'd never have got through them all. On the outer checkpoints, every vehicle's been carefully scrutinized — both outside and in.'

Brand was staring fixedly at the wall-map. He said, 'Just the same, the girl has got out. Though not by road.'

Even policemen are human. And Walford had been losing sleep. He said with heavy sarcasm, 'I suppose she borrowed a helicopter?'

Brand considered the idea. 'No . . . no, I don't think so . . . ' Walford snorted. Brand said: 'I wasn't thinking of air . . . I was thinking of water.'

Now Walford snorted more loudly than ever. 'The Thames Division are watching the river.'

Then Brand's right hand moved. His index finger extended. It touched the wall-map. It traced the path of a thin, wavering blue line. 'Not the roads, Len,' he said. 'Not the river. *A canal.*'

Walford stared at him.

'A canal,' Brand insisted. 'That must be

the answer. There's no other explanation left!'

And Walford sucked in his breath.

'You could be right, Brand. Hell's bells — that's one thing I hadn't thought of! And the canals are quiet and secluded . . . not much traffic on them at this time of year . . . '

He was moving.

'The boatmen are the sort to mind their own business, even if they bother to read a newspaper . . . '

He had reached a phone. He lifted it urgently. 'Get me the Inland Waterways Executive,' he said. 'Commander Walford here. Hurry it up!'

He covered the phone's mouthpiece, and swung his head to tell Brand: 'I'll get all the lock-keepers alerted to watch out for her.'

But maybe it won't be that easy, Brand thought. Doll Winters had had a good start, and the canals wandered all over the country. She might be anywhere by now . . .

And he wondered: had the killer been brighter than they were? Had he already picked up her trail?

★ ★ ★

Fred Baron's bad tooth was acting up again. He held the *Phoebe's* wheel with one hand and his jaw with the other. From time to time he muttered under his breath: 'Sadists . . . '

Doll's sympathy was tinged with impatience. 'You ought to have it pulled out, Fred. Why don't we stop somewhere and you go into town and see a dentist? I'm sure that's the thing to do.'

'I'll be all right,' he mumbled. 'It'll leave off after a bit.'

'Really, anyone would think you were scared! A grown man, too — making a fuss about having a tooth out.'

'I'm not — ' Fred's face screwed up in sudden agony as another twinge shot through him. 'Hell, it's giving me gyp!'

Doll Winters said no more. Was this the man she was going to marry? Was he a man? Or a mouse? She had to work hard to build her romance out of such material . . .

Then she had something else to occupy her mind. Another lock coming up ahead.

A weir reached across the width of the canal, damming the water in the pound. It was a running weir, with surplus water cascading over and down to a lower level. They were descending now.

She stared at the narrow lock chamber set in one side of the weir . . . Fred had shown her how to work locks, and this was an opportunity for her to show him that she could do it on her own. She ran over the operation in her mind.

The lock gates were already open to receive them, so all she had to do was to lean on the balance beam to close the gates after the *Phoebe* had entered. Then she must use the windlass to wind down the paddles and close the sluices and, after that, walk forward to the lower set of gates and raise the paddles to let the water out of the lock chamber so that the boat would gradually settle down to the lower level. Simple. That done, all that would remain would be to lean on the beam to open the far gates.

She climbed atop the low cabin, ready to jump ashore with the windlass. Glancing back, she saw a big light-blue cruiser coming up fast astern. There were two men aboard it, and she read the name on the hull: *The Hunter*.

'Let 'em go first,' Fred said carelessly. 'We're in no hurry.'

He swung the wheel over so that the *Phoebe* drifted towards the weir, and waved the other boat through. As it headed towards the lock, Doll found herself staring at one of the two men aboard. A man uncoiling a mooring line. He wore a navy blue jacket with brass buttons . . .

Suddenly, he tossed his line at Doll and called: 'Hold fast!'

Doll, standing on top of the cabin, caught the line without thinking. She was still wondering where she had seen the man before. There was something strangely familiar about that long, mournful face. But before she got round to mentally placing a bowler hat over it, he gave a sharp jerk on the line.

Doll was pulled off-balance. She fell from the cabin roof, arms flailing wildly, and hit the water with a splash. She bobbed up, spitting, screaming: 'Fred!'

Then the current caught hold of her and swept her towards the weir. She went under again. A foaming torrent tossed her about, carried her over the weir . . . down into the surging maelstrom below.

★   ★   ★

Nick Chandler fought his way up through clinging shrouds of darkness. The blackness seemed to waver, and he realized this was due to a faint grey light filtering down through cracks in the ceiling. Nick wondered where he was. His head pounded like a steam-hammer, and the air reeked of petroleum.

He began to remember: he had been attacked by two men behind G. Dodd's Car Mart — and consciousness fully returned. It was not his head that was vibrating. The sound came from a nearby compressor. He lay, bound and gagged, at the bottom of an inspection pit, covered over with heavy timbers.

Nick wriggled into a sitting position, back against one concrete wall, and filled his lungs with air. He strained at the

185

cords holding him without making an impression on them. How long had he been unconscious, he wondered.

The situation was bad. Dodd, without doubt, was running with the car thieves — might even perhaps be the killer. The thought roused Nick to a sense of danger. Brand had no idea where he was . . . so he had only himself to rely on if he were to escape. And there was Doll Winters to consider . . . her life hung by a thread and the sooner he broadcast his new knowledge the better.

He considered what he knew about inspection pits. Mechanics were not the most careful of workmen. He could hope to find some discarded tool down here, if he were lucky. In the darkness, he began to wriggle about the floor of the pit, fingers groping in an inch of oily muck.

He located a sliver of metal and explored it by touch. A part of a hacksaw blade. Nick grinned, blessing the carelessness of one garage mechanic. He forced one end of the sliver of metal between the cord binding his ankles, and rested the other end against the wall. Head bent over, he rubbed his bound wrists up and down across the worn, broken teeth of the fragment of blade. He worked steadily, despite aching muscles . . . the blade slipped again and again, and time passed and the cord around his wrists didn't even seem to be fraying. It was a long, frustrating job.

His limbs were numb from the tightness of the cord, and the blade grazed his flesh till his wrists were raw and bleeding. He stuck at it, sawing away for what seemed like hours, and finally he made an impression. He flexed his arms and strained with every ounce of his strength — and the cord snapped.

He pulled the gag from his mouth and set to work to saw through the cord round his ankles then. That did not take long. He stood up, braced his body, and pushed at one of the heavy planks overhead.

It moved an inch, then another inch, and he looked out. He saw a line of cars and, beyond them, men drinking tea in a small office.

Nick pushed hard at the plank, sliding

it forward. He reached up and hauled himself out through the narrow opening, darting a quick look around. No one had seen him. He replaced the plank over the pit and walked quickly away.

He walked to the front of the garage where his Jaguar waited beside the pumps. The attendant seemed only mildly curious about the state of his clothes and his wrists, and the fact that he came from inside the garage. This man must be just a casual worker here, Nick guessed. He wouldn't be in on the stolen car racket.

'All, ready for you, sir,' the attendant said. 'There's no fault that we can detect.'

'Thanks.' Nick reached for an inside pocket, praying that he still had his wallet. 'One of those things, I suppose.' His wallet hadn't been taken from him, and it was intact. He tipped the attendant generously. He slid behind the wheel of the Jaguar. 'I used to know a couple of people here,' he said casually. 'A man with rather sad face . . . always wore a bowler . . . '

'That would be the boss. Mr. Dodd.'

' . . . And a man with tattooed hands,

and odd-coloured eyes?'

'Don Westerly, the foreman.'

Nick lifted his eyes to heaven. Handed to him on a plate! 'Either of them around now?' he asked.

The attendant shook his head. 'You just missed them. They left together just as you arrived.'

And then Nick remembered the black saloon. He breathed hard. 'Can you tell me where Mr. Dodd lives?'

'Yes sir. It's just around the corner — not a hundred yards from here.' And he pointed. 'The big house with green tiles.'

'Thanks again,' Nick said, and drove off. He found the house easily, parked outside it, and studied it. The door of the garage was open. The garage was visibly empty. So the odds were against Dodd being at home.

He went up to the house, and pressed the bell push. Chimes sounded, and presently a blonde woman opened the door. She was young, and pretty in a blowsy sort of way. She looked as if she had been crying. Her eyes were puffy and red.

'Mrs. Dodd?' Nick said.

'Yes.'

The woman was staring, but not at Nick's well-nigh ruined clothes. She was regarding him fixedly, tremulously, looking up into his face as if expecting to see something terrible there.

'Mr. Dodd . . . is he in?' Nick said, and the woman's lips shook. The corners of her mouth dragged abruptly down.

'He isn't here,' she said, and her voice wavered. 'He — ' She broke off her eyes suddenly filling with tears. She swung away from him blindly. 'You — you'd better come in. I — I've just made some more tea. I — '

She said no more. She stumbled back down the hall. And after hesitating for a moment, Nick followed.

He followed her into a long, L-shaped living room that was luxuriously carpeted and expensively furnished. There were toys on the floor near a telephone beside a bay window, but no other signs of a child.

There was a tea tray on a table: teapot, milk jug, sugar bowl, one cup and saucer.

Dodd's wife stood beside it, her back to Nick, her shoulders hunched forward. She splashed tea into the cup with an unsteady hand She got out: 'You — you know Gerald?'

So that was what the 'G' stood for, Nick thought, and wondered what was going on here. He said: 'Yes, I know him.' And, in a way, it was true.

He thought: By their deeds, ye shall know them . . .

He said: 'Yes, I know your husband. Can you tell me where I can find him?'

And, suddenly, she completely broke down.

'He's gone!' she sobbed. 'Gone away! With — with another woman — !'

Nick stared. Another woman? It didn't seem likely. 'Do you know where he's gone?'

Mrs. Dodd's racking sobs hung on the air. 'He — he wouldn't be likely to tell me would he? Me, left with a kid on my hands. All dressed up like — like a weekend sailor, he was. Got his fancy piece aboard a boat somewhere — '

A boat! Nick felt sorry for the blonde

wife of Gerald Dodd. She didn't seem to know her husband as well as he himself already knew him. Everything was adding up. Gerald Dodd's wife was going to be badly hurt.

He put a hand on her shoulder to comfort her but, still sobbing she swung away from him. She left him there. She blundered out of the room. He heard her on the stairs.

Gravely, he looked around.

He saw a framed photograph on a sideboard: a picture of a man a woman, and a young boy. He picked it up.

The woman in the picture was blonde — Mrs. Dodd. The man was long-faced and mournful — no doubting who *he* was, not for a minute. The boy in the picture physically favoured his father. Nick hoped for the boy's sake, that the likeness was only skin-deep.

The framed photograph in his hand, he moved to the living room.

He could still hear Mrs. Dodd sobbing: crying as if her heart would break. She was somewhere upstairs.

Nick slowly turned around again then,

and crossed the room to pick up the phone. He began to dial.

* * *

Fear washed through Doll Winters as she went over the weir. She fell through a cataract of water, down and down. It boiled and surged about her as she was carried along, helplessly, by the current. She went under again, spluttering and frightened.

The killer had found her . . . she was drowning! Shock stifled her ability to think clearly and she struggled instinctively, futilely. Oh, why had she never learned to swim, she thought desperately. Probably because she'd never had anyone to teach her.

Her lungs filled with water and she sank, struck something solid and tried to hold on, failed, and was swept submerged through a grey world of water where rubbish and rusty tins congregated.

This was the end, she thought . . . she couldn't last must longer . . .

Then she felt strong arms about her.

He had got her, was holding her under! She fought like a tigress and her head bobbed above water and she gulped in air.

A voice said: 'Stop fighting me, Doll!'

Through a blur of mist she saw Fred Baron's homely face. It was Fred Baron who held her. She relaxed. Good old Fred . . . Fred to the rescue.

She gave up struggling and let him tow her to the side.

He dragged her out of the water and they lay, side by side on the canal bank, panting. Neither of them spoke. Then Fred sat up. He took his pipe from his mouth and cleaned the bowl, rammed fresh tobacco into it, and tried to strike wet matches. He gave up after the third attempt and said gently: 'You're a silly girl, Doll. You didn't have to take that line.'

And, after saying it, he considered it.

'That chap must have been crazy,' he said, 'throwing you a line like that — no point to it. It's the sort of thing that causes accidents.'

Doll had partially recovered from her

ordeal. She shivered. 'It was no accident Fred! It was no accident, Fred! It was him — the killer, I mean. I'm sure of it!'

Fred looked at her. 'You're not making this up?'

Doll shook her head, and Fred Baron rose to his feet and stared hard at the lock. The *Hunter* had passed through and was heading up the canal at top speed. It was already almost out of sight. 'Well, he's gone now,' he said slowly.

A cyclist on the towpath across the narrow waterway called. 'You all right? Want any help?'

'We're okay, thanks,' Fred answered.

'I saw what happened,' the cyclist said. 'That fellow ought to be reported. He rode off, grumbling about the carelessness of landlubbers who should never be allowed in boats.

'I've got to get away from here,' Doll muttered. 'He'll come back for me.'

Fred Baron held her hand. 'Don't worry, Doll — I'll know him again. I'll look after you . . . come on, let's get back aboard our boat.'

They walked along the bank to the

Phoebe, and Fred Baron handed Doll back on board. He swung the wheel, so that the boat headed back the way they had come. 'I know a trick to beat him ... there's an abandoned branch canal we passed half a mile back. We can force a way through, and he'll never guess where we are.'

Doll Winters threw her arms round his neck and kissed him. 'Oh Fred, you are wonderful!'

Fred grunted. 'You'd better get below and change, Doll.'

The *Phoebe* surged forward; slowed after a time as he watched the banks. 'About here, somewhere ... ' Willows screened the opening, and rushes and weeds choked the waterway.

Fred Baron turned the nose of the boat in, and gave it full throttle. The backwater was narrow, with bushes and branches hanging down on each side; a secret place; shallow, with a pebbly bottom. He had not gone far before he had to stop and clear the screw of weeds.

He went on again, and reached an ancient lock. The mechanism was rusted and stiff from disuse, and though Doll had now reappeared on deck and was helping, it took him a long time to work their way through. Then they had to stop again, to clear more weed off the screw.

'Never mind Doll,' Fred said cheerfully. 'That louse'll hardly think to look for us along here!'

The *Phoebe* penetrated an overgrown canal in the middle of nowhere, isolated from roads and houses and people. She travelled slowly and inexorably towards her fate.

14

Face To Face

Gerald Dodd sweated. His hands trembled as he poured another large measure of whisky into a glass and gulped it down. His nerves had been shot to pieces since his failure to silence the girl at the lock.

'Better go easy on that stuff, boss,' Westerly said, afraid of him falling apart.

'I'm okay,' Dodd snarled. 'That damn cyclist! If he hadn't turned up just when he did, we could have killed both of 'em!'

His fingers curled around the butt of the revolver in his pocket. Only one thing for it now. Time's running out.' He pulled the gun from his pocket and flourished it.

Westerly said, 'For Pete's sake, Mr. Dodd! Put that thing away.' He swung the *Hunter* round and headed back for the lock when it became clear that the *Phoebe* wasn't following. But the lock was empty, and the *Phoebe* had gone. He continued down the canal towards London, and still there was no sign of the other boat. 'They turned off somewhere,' he said, disgusted.

Dodd unfolded a map of the canal system and peered at it blearily. He stabbed a finger. 'There! A disused channel — see? After them, Don!'

Westerly turned the *Hunter* again, watching the bankside. He found the entrance to the derelict cut and steered for it.

'Got 'em now!' Dodd gloated, pouring himself another drink. 'Got 'em trapped!'

'Lay off that whisky, Mr. Dodd,' Westerly said curtly. 'You need a clear head for what's coming . . . '

'I need another drink!'

The *Hunter* passed under the overhanging boughs and forced a passage through long stretches of weed. The going was easier than Westerly had expected. He said: 'They're clearing a way for us. And they can't be travelling as fast as we are.'

They passed through a lock, and then a hillside towered over them. The black opening of a tunnel showed. The canal went straight into the hill. Westerly steered at the black hole . . .

An arch of slimy bricks closed over their heads. Water dropped from the walls. The air was clammy and smelt of decay. Hollow echoes reverberated the whole length of the tunnel.

Westerly lit a cigarette, and the brief flare of the match illuminated Gerald Dodd's unshaven face, a bottle tilted at his mouth. 'You hear what I hear?' Westerly asked.

'Wha'sat?'

The sound of a second engine throbbed through the tunnel. 'They're not far ahead,' said Westerly.

'Good!' Dodd pulled out his gun. 'Finish 'em off in here, and nobody will ever know.' He saw red beady eyes watching him from a brick ledge. 'Leave 'em down here for the rats!'

Westerly fed some more power to the engine, and the *Hunter* surged forward. Ahead, outlined against the daylight at the far end of the tunnel, was the shape of a motor cruiser . . .

'That's them!' Dodd leaned forward, eager. 'Get closer!' He'd shut that girl's mouth this time, he thought. She wouldn't get away again. He'd get close, and make sure. Quite sure. 'Faster!' he urged.

The wash from the boat rebounded from the tunnel walls and creamed into foam. Gerald Dodd stared into the gloom, finger tightening on the trigger of his gun. He saw the stern of the *Phoebe*, and the dark shape of a human figure. He fired. The sound of the shot echoed and re-echoed through the long tunnel.

He fired again.

★　★　★

In his office overlooking the Thames Embankment, Deputy-Commander Walford sat waiting for the telephone to ring.

The tea in the cup on his desk was cold, and grey smoke spiralled upwards from the cigarette clenched between his fingers. He had forgotten it. Now he crushed out the butt, and sighed wearily.

Waiting played havoc with the nerves,

he reflected. And so much of police routine was waiting . . . just waiting.

He had alerted the canal authorities, and it could now only be a question of time before he heard something from them. And yet he sat and worried. The canal system was a labyrinth covering the entire country; and so many of the waterways were abandoned — yet passable for small craft. Impossible to check every branch . . .

He worried for the girl, Winters.

A phone pealed once before he hooked it off the cradle and rapped: 'Walford.'

'Chandler here. Is the chief there? I rang our office, and Miss Rington said he was at the Yard.'

Walford frowned. 'No, he isn't. I don't know where he is — gone off on some caper of his own. He wouldn't tell me where he was going.' He tried to remember Brand's exact words —

'I'm taking up that idea of yours, Len . . . '

What idea had that been, Walford wondered. He was irritated. Brand had an annoying habit of talking in mysteries.

There was something in the private detective's make-up that made him reluctant to speak out before he was ready. He was usually right in the end. Though it could be hard on the people working with him.

Walford said, exasperation in his voice, 'If you've got a lead, Nick, let's have it. I don't have to tell you that it's your duty to help the police.'

'Of course not, Len . . . ' Nick's voice was honeyed. 'I've identified the men you want . . . Gerald Dodd, of London Road, Norbury, and his foreman, Don Westerly. I've got a picture of Dodd. And if you raid his garage you'll find that hot car depot that you've been looking for.'

Walford breathed more easily and scribbled notes as Nick gave details. Maybe, this time, he would steal a march on Brand . . .

'Right Nick, I'll take over from here. I'll arrange for the local Division to raid the garage, and I'll put out a call for Westerly and Dodd. Your identification will help a lot — and thanks for your co-operation.'

'Any news your end?' Nick asked.

Walford hesitated. Then he relented. 'We've picked up their black Rover Saloon at Uxbridge. They're on the canals somewhere . . . '

*   *   *

Somewhere a bird hovered. A metal bird.

Simon Brand focused his binoculars and studied the landscape unwinding beneath him as his pilot took the helicopter along the route of the Grand Union canal.

Walford's remark, intended as sarcasm — *'I suppose she borrowed a helicopter?'* — had put an idea into his head.

Pursuit by water was not practical. There were too many locks to negotiate, and a strict speed limit to be observed on all canals to avoid damage to the banks. Roads only occasionally crossed the canals, and the towpaths were hardly suited to fast driving, even where they existed at all.

A helicopter was the only practical way of covering such a network of waterways, and so Brand had hired one.

His eyes searched out the boats idly scattered along the Grand Union now. He had not much hope here. By now, he realized, the people he was looking for must have turned into one of the branch canals — or a lock-keeper would have spotted them. And there were many disused branches, remote from habitation, that were still passable . . .

Hovering like a hawk in the air, its rotor a shimmering silver circle, the helicopter roared on . . . a chequerboard of woods and farms and meadows spread out below, tinted golden-brown by the autumn sunlight. Brand watched the land through the perspex window of the cabin.

He wondered about Nick. If anything had happened to his young partner, he thought, he'd . . . he put the thought from him. Somewhere below, a defenceless girl fled in terror before two determined killers, at least one of them armed. He hunted a light-blue cruiser, wondering how much time he had.

He tapped the pilot on the shoulder, and pointed. Like a silver thread, a derelict cut wound through a tangle of woodland and disappeared under a hill. 'We'll try that one,' he said tersely.

The pilot took the helicopter up, over the hill. And then Brand saw the aqueduct.

It had been built more than a hundred years before, perhaps by one of the great engineers of the canal era, Brindley or Telford; a dead straight channel of water, gleaming silver in the sun, crossing the chasm that fell away seventy feet below.

The aqueduct was a metal trough, both shallow and narrow — restricting passage to one direction at a time — and constructed of cast-iron sections poised on massive stone arches. It was more than a thousand feet long and in the days of its construction it had been a considerable achievement. In its time it had seen a regular service of gaily-painted narrow boats . . .

But now the ironwork was rusted and the masonry was beginning to crumble away in places. Rarely did even a pleasure boat seek out this remote branch of the waterways. Its stark grandeur had weathered to merge with the soft contours of the surrounding countryside, so that it appeared one with the wooded valley and the stream rippling over stones like pigeon's eggs far below.

Yet it could still be traversed. The engineers had built well, and the aqueduct waited now, spanning the steep-sided chasm, still holding its precious water.

And soon a boat would come again to renew, however briefly, the purpose for which the aqueduct had been built.

★　★　★

'Keep your head down, Doll,' Fred Baron said grimly.

Bullets whined along the tunnel and ricocheted off the dank, slimy walls. They were deep under the hill, and the *Hunter* was gaining on them. Doll Winters felt the *Phoebe* rock as Fred Baron opened the engine out to its fastest speed.

She crouched low, watching the path of daylight ahead. *He* had found her again and, this time, there could be no escape.

She shivered. She chewed on a handkerchief.

Fred said: 'I'm going as fast as I can,
Doll. If we can reach a lock in time, I'll
try draining it to maroon them.'

Doll didn't understand what he meant,
but she knew it no longer mattered. The
killer was right behind her, and there was
no time to work a rusty, antiquated lock.
She was trapped, and she couldn't even
get out and run . . .

The clammy brick walls of the tunnel
seemed to press in on her. She saw the
red eyes of rats in the darkness. She
couldn't swim, and there was nowhere to
hide. She felt sorry for Fred, though. The
killer wouldn't leave him alive.

A tear crawled down her cheeks. It was
just like the films. So romantic! They'd
found true love and they would die
together . . . only she didn't want to die,
not now she'd found someone to live for.

The tunnel ended, and she blinked in
bright sunshine. And there lay the
aqueduct, a narrow bridge of water high
above a sheer-sided chasm. Doll's heart
sank. It was a bad place to be caught.

The *Hunter* was close behind as they started out across the aqueduct. Doll looked down with a shudder. She felt giddy. Who'd have imagined that there could be water right up here? It wasn't sense, she thought wildly. Canals were supposed to stay on the ground. She felt terrified.

'Take the wheel, Doll,' Fred muttered. 'Keep going. Fast as you can. Don't stop for anything.'

Doll obeyed, watching him pick up a windlass and heft it in his hand. Her eyes opened wide. 'What are you doing, Fred?' She glanced back as he clambered on to the stern . . . and the *Hunter* was only a couple of feet behind now and she saw its hard prow and the bitter-eyed face of the man at the wheel . . . and the killer, standing beside him, reloading his gun and swearing.

'Keep her steady,' Fred called. 'You haven't a lot of clearance.'

That was true, Doll thought, and concentrated. The rusting sides of the metal trough almost scraped the *Phoebe's* hull. Doll avoided looking down.

Fred Baron balanced on the stern, sweating. He had only a desperate chance, and he knew it. But he had to do something to protect this hunted, frightened girl, Doll Winters.

He jumped, and he landed sprawling on the *Hunter's* hull.

He scrambled forward to the cockpit, and began laying about him with the windlass.

15

Nemesis

Westerly saw Fred Baron coming, and nudged Todd in the ribs. 'Here, grab the wheel! I'll take care of this boy!'

Gerald Dodd looked up in alarm. He wished he hadn't drunk so much. He wished he hadn't emptied his revolver in the tunnel. Above all, he wished he'd never got involved with murder . . .

'Hurry it up!' Westerly said sharply — and Gerald Dodd hurried.

Westerly hadn't much confidence in his boss in a fight, and he didn't fancy losing control over a boat perched seventy feet above the ground. He spat on his hands and waited. 'Keep her straight, and don't lose the girl,' he ordered.

Fred Baron came in swinging the heavy metal windlass as a club. Westerly pitied him. This boy had obviously never been in a rough house before. He was green.

Westerly ducked under the wildly swinging windlass and launched tattooed fists into the pit of Fred Baron's stomach. The air woofed out of Fred's lungs. Westerly booted the younger man's ankles, and Fred Baron went crashing down. As he did so, Westerly grabbed for the windlass and wrenched it away. He aimed a blow at Fred's head with it.

The younger man managed to roll. The windless only struck him glancingly. But it still dazed him. More by instinct than anything else, he got his arms round Westerly's legs. Somehow, he had to save Doll. Westerly tried to kick his way free, but went off balance as Gerald swung the wheel of the boat drunkenly and erratically. He cursed as he fell. But the fall broke Fred Baron's hold.

'Now!' Westerly snarled, lunging for the younger man and fastening his hands on his throat; squeezing.

Fred Baron gave a strangled cry, and kicked out. He was lucky . . . One of his knees jolted into Westerly's groin, crippling him.

The two men rolled over and over,

inextricably entangled, neither capable of finishing the other . . .

Doll Winters was screaming. Fred was fighting to save her! It was just like the cinema . . . though she had a sneaking feeling she ought not to be running away. A real heroine would be in there, fighting alongside her man.

But as the *Hunter* was right behind her and travelling fast, it could not be said that she was running to any purpose. The two boats reached the centre of the high aqueduct . . . and then she heard Fred Baron cry out.

He was in trouble! Without thinking, Doll cut the engine. And the *Hunter* rammed the *Phoebe's* stern. Doll was knocked sideways. The two boats jammed together in the narrow trough.

Doll scrambled back on to her feet. She dived into the cabin and jerked out again with a carving knife in her hand and a gleam in her eyes. No one was going to hurt her Fred! She saw the long-faced killer clambering unsteadily over the stern, gun in hand, coming for her . . . there was no sign of

Fred or the other man.

She waited, knife ready. She could smell the whisky on the killer's breath. As he made a grab for her, she stabbed wildly. The blade was deflected by the barrel of the killer's gun. He made a grab for her, fastened a hand on her.

'*Got you — you — !*'

At that moment, the two boats began to drift apart, and the movement caught Dodd and Doll unawares. Doll staggered off-balance, and fell. She made a grab for the iron frame of the trough and hung there, half in and half out of the water, as the *Phoebe* slid away from beneath her.

The next instant, Gerald Dodd sprang.

He got one hand on the frame. He fastened the other on Doll Winter's shoulder. He wrenched her upwards and outwards. He wrenched her out of the water, and over the edge of the aqueduct.

And then he threw her out into space.

Doll Winters was falling. And screaming. This was the end of her.

Seventy feet below, jagged-toothed rocks waited to tear the life out of her body.

Her hands flailed as she fell.

And then those hands hit one of the girders supporting the aqueduct. Hit it and, somehow, held on.

And there she hung by her fingertips, and she was still screaming.

There she hung, with certain death waiting for her far below in the imminent future.

Already, her fingers were starting to slip.

★   ★   ★

'Get down there!' Simon Brand rapped. 'Go on, man! Get down there fast!'

Tight-lipped, Brand's pilot nodded. And the helicopter dropped, like a hawk on its prey.

Brand wished he'd packed his Luger, but he'd set out to find a girl on the run, and a gun hadn't seemed necessary. Now he bitterly regretted that error of judgment.

The scene below riveted his gaze. It was dramatic. The high iron bridge, poised on stone arches, and the two small motor cruisers in the middle of the narrow strip of water . . . and the young girl hanging from the lowest girder beneath the rim of the aqueduct, hanging on for her life above a sheer drop, while a gunman slowly inched his way downwards to reach her.

Brand saw it all clearly. Could he intervene in time to save Doll Winters's life? She hung by her fingertips and the gunman was bent on dislodging her tenuous hold.

Brand went into action.

As the helicopter swooped down, so he jerked open the cabin door and kicked out the short flexible ladder. The next moment, he was on the ladder, the wind whipping at him. He climbed down it swiftly, and then he tensed, ready for what he knew he must do . . .

That was when the man with the gun heard the roar of the helicopter's engine overhead, and shot a startled glance upwards. Then he froze. He hesitated between going on down over the girders to finish the girl off and dealing with the lean figure on the ladder now swooping down on him.

He hesitated only a moment. Then his gun came up sharply — to throw lead at Brand.

Simon Brand didn't hesitate very long, either, despite the fact that he knew that an error of more than a couple of inches in what he was about to attempt to do would certainly result in his death — even if the gunman below him didn't account for him first.

Some of the bullets were whining dangerously close. One ripped at his jacket as it flapped in the wind.

He dropped down over the remaining rungs of the ladder; gripped the bottom rung for an instant; then let himself go.

He fell like a stone.

Then for one long, quite dreadful second, that seemed to stretch into an eternity, he was left wondering as he plummeted downwards through space. Had he miscalculated? Would his be the first broken body on the rocks below?

The rim of the aqueduct flashed past his eyes. Now was the time. Now! He threw his arms forward. The next moment, as his hands clamped down on girder, he felt as if his arms would be pulled clean out of their sockets. But, the instant after that, he knew he had made it. He had arrested his fall. He coiled like a spring. He swung himself up.

He was on a girder eighty feet above boulder-strewn ground. A narrow girder.

And not more than ten yards away from him, holding on with one hand, blazing gun in the other, there was the man whom Blake had been looking forward to coming to grips with for what seemed like a very long time.

Now they met face to face high above the jagged-toothed rocks, where the slightest miscalculation or slip could mean death for either, or both, of them.

Now they met face to face — with Doll Winters desperately hanging on to life by her fingertips eight foot beneath them.

Now they met face to face — Simon Brand, and the killer.

And Simon Brand instantly started to move again.

He went the only way that he knew; and he went fast.

He went forward.

And Gerald Dodd, seeing him coming, emptied his gun at him, screaming curses. Bullets howled off into space. Others whanged into metal. But Brand kept on coming, and coming fast.

There was nothing more likely to destroy the aim of any man with a gun than to charge straight at him. This Simon Brand knew. Give the gunman no time to aim. Give him no time even to think.

Lead snarled all around Brand, but he didn't falter.

And the trick worked for him again, as it had so often worked in the past. The gunman was flustered. Badly flustered. So badly flustered that he couldn't shoot straight.

But Brand didn't even begin to guess just how flustered Gerald Dodd really was.

Dodd had been living on the knife-edge of his nerves for days past. Nothing had gone right for him. And the whisky he'd gulped to give himself courage made his head reel and blurred his vision. Sweat ran out of his face like water as he fired and fired and fired again — uselessly. Then Brand was upon him.

And now Dodd's gun was empty. But still, desperately, he used it as a weapon as he wrestled with Brand on the narrow girder poised over eighty feet of near-empty air.

And he managed to slash out with the gun. The barrel raked Brand's head from temple to jawbone, momentarily dazing the detective. He staggered; almost fell. But it was death to fall, and he knew it Somehow, he regained his balance and bloodied the long face in front of him with a right uppercut. The gun barrel swung at him again.

Brand chopped the gun out of the other man's hand, and uppercut him again. He punished Dodd. And then Gerald Dodd knew that he had no chance of winning this battle. Fighting on equal terms, Brand could and would take him apart. And he started to scramble away from the detective.

Then he saw Doll Winters clinging desperately to the girder eight feet below him.

That blasted girl! He'd forgotten all about her — and yet he shouldn't have forgotten all about her. This was all her fault! Damn her to hell, she'd ruined everything . . .

He knew what he was going to do. No matter what happened, he was going to kill her . . . *now!* His eyes red-rimmed and glaring with the light of near madness, he jumped for the girder below.

He never reached it.

For as he jumped, hell-bent on kicking the girl off into space, so Brand made a grab for him. And Gerald Dodd twisted in air to evade the detective's grasp.

Brand didn't touch him. Nobody touched him. He did it himself. That wrenching twist in mid-air did it. He missed the girder below.

He went backwards straight out into space, He plummeted downwards, arms wide and legs wide, lips pulled back over his teeth in a long drawn-out scream.

Then Dodd hit the rocks. It seemed to be an eternity later.

And then there was silence.

★   ★   ★

Doll Winters was near to fainting. Desperately she wondered how much longer she could hold on for. All the time her fingers were slipping. She could feel them slipping.

Her eyes were tight shut.

She dared not look up and see her fingers slipping nearer and ever nearer to the edge of the girder from which she hung. She dared not look down. She had heard the dreadful scream plunging away into the chasm below her, and she knew what it meant. Fear made her sick. Already the rocks below her had claimed one victim. Would she be next?

And then suddenly she felt strong hands close about her wrists, and heard a persuasive voice above her. 'Relax now, Miss Winters. I've got you.'

She opened her eyes then and looked up into a friendly, lean, hard-muscled face. There was something infinitely reassuring about the strong lines of that face. Doll instantly knew, and knew instinctively, that she had nothing more to worry about.

'Up you come now!' he said. And, with infinite care, he drew her up until she could stand on the girder beside him. 'Don't look down, Miss Winters . . . ' She had stiffened and shivered. 'I've got you. You're all right.'

A helicopter whirred overhead, like some gigantic clattering clockwork toy. A steel hawser that terminated in a leather harness slid down.

'I'm going to buckle you into this harness,' the man said. 'Then the helicopter will lift us together . . .

'I'm Simon Brand,' he continued quietly, as he worked on the harness straps. 'You came to my office for help, remember? To you, that must seem a long time ago now.'

'I remember,' Doll said, excited. The private eye! She began to dream again. He didn't look middle-aged, not really. And he was handsome, too . . .

She smiled.

Then she remembered Marla Dean, his blonde secretary, and the smile faded. A willowy honey-blonde straight off the cover of a glossy magazine. It wasn't fair.

Being stranded on a girder in mid-air had destroyed her sense of reality and paralyzed her memory. Now it all came back to her. Fred! Where was he? She glanced anxiously upwards.

'Fred!' she called anxiously. 'You all right?'

She had to shout to be heard above the din the helicopter was making.

Then the homely face of Fred Baron appeared over the edge of the aqueduct, craning down. 'Is that you, Doll? Doll, is that you?'

'Yes, it's me, Fred. Fred . . . you all right, Fred?'

'Doll! Thank God, you're safe! I nearly went out of my mind! I — I settled this one's hash, Doll.'

'Fred! Darling!' she called back. Then, more sharply, 'Fred — you're hurt . . . '

And Fred Baron did look a trifle battered.

Brand finished buckling Doll Winters into the leather harness, then grasped the wire hawser firmly, and waved to the helicopter's pilot. 'Haul away!' he shouted.

And, little more than a minute later, after more bellowed instructions, the helicopter's pilot deposited both Brand and Doll Winters on the deck of the *Hunter*.

Once there, Brand paused only for long enough to free Doll Winters from her harness, and then went quickly forward to take charge of the man with the odd-coloured eyes. Fred Baron had done a good job on him. He lay on the floor of the cockpit with an egg-sized swelling on his skull, and he looked as if he might sleep for a month.

Doll clambered past to get at Fred Baron who was holding his jaw. 'Knocked my tooth out,' he mumbled. 'The bad one.'

'Poor Fred . . . ' she clucked over him. Then she brightened. 'Still it's lucky it was the bad one . . . ' But she still managed to sound most sympathetic.

Something had changed Doll Winters of Tooting Bec. She stopped dreaming about romance. Firmly, quite sure of herself, she said: 'You need a woman to look after you, Fred Baron. I think I'd better take you in hand. I think I'd better marry you.'

He looked happy enough at the prospect. 'It's all right with me, Doll.'

As they came together, like a pair of lovebirds, Simon Brand smiled and turned away. Brand knew when he wasn't wanted.

★   ★   ★

Down on the farm, Arnie the Ape was reading the *Daily Post*. He read slowly, dwelling on the lead story. And it seemed from what he read that he no longer had a problem.

He didn't have to squeal on anyone. The girl was safe. He felt happy about that. Arnie Bendix was a harmless sort and he wouldn't want a nice young girl to get hurt . . .

But now he had another problem, Mr. Gerald Dodd was dead, and the job Dodd had promised Arnie Bendix had died with him.

Arnie looked up from the paper he was reading. He looked across the polished table and the vase of flowers to the neat, red-lipped widow. There was a log fire burning in the grate behind her, and a vista of rolling farmland through the window.

Arnie Bendix's face screwed up in a wistful expression. 'I suppose,' he blurted out, 'I suppose I couldn't just stay on here?'

The woman looked at him. She smiled. 'Of course you can, Mr. Bendix. I think I'd like that . . . '

★   ★   ★

Murder leaves an aftermath that rarely makes the headlines.

Murderers, too, leave families and relatives and friends — and these are the ultimate sufferers, along with the families and relatives and friends of the victim.

Janet Dodd was staying with her sister, a long way from the house in Norbury. Nick had considerately arranged that . . .

There was a deep-felt hurt feeling inside Janet Dodd: a wound that would take a long time to heal. There was numbness, a dull ache and regret. She felt that in some way she had failed Gerald.

The tears had dried now, but her face was blank and her movements automatic. Something important had died within her. The police had been polite and tactful, and she had remembered to hide the newspapers from the child.

At twenty-eight, life was not over. It could go on a long time yet, and every second of every day she would remember. She understood too well now. If only it had been another woman . . .

The young Paul looked up from his jigsaw, puzzled. 'But, Mum, where's Dad gone . . . ?'

She turned slowly to face him, consciously composing her features. Thank God she'd hidden the papers! 'Don't worry about it, Paul. I'll tell you all about it one day . . . want me to help with that jigsaw puzzle?'

'Oh . . . all right,' the boy said reluctantly.

She tried to find the pieces, but they all looked alike. They all looked like the face of her dead husband.

She wondered when she would tell her son, Paul, the truth — the whole truth. And she wondered how she would tell him.

It wouldn't be easy.

Just how do you tell your son that his father was a murderer . . . ?

No . . . it wouldn't be easy at all.

THE END

We do hope that you have enjoyed reading this large print book.

Did you know that all of our titles are available for purchase?

We publish a wide range of high quality large print books including:
Romances, Mysteries, Classics General Fiction Non Fiction and Westerns

Special interest titles available in large print are:
The Little Oxford Dictionary Music Book, Song Book Hymn Book, Service Book

Also available from us courtesy of Oxford University Press:
Young Readers' Dictionary (large print edition) Young Readers' Thesaurus (large print edition)

For further information or a free brochure, please contact us at:
Ulverscroft Large Print Books Ltd., The Green, Bradgate Road, Anstey, Leicester, LE7 7FU, England.
Tel: (00 44) **0116 236 4325**
Fax: (00 44) **0116 234 0205**

WORKHOUSE PROPHECY

Pam Littlewood

At Beesthorpe Hall an attic room has been locked for fifty years. In 1875, Wilhelmina the laundry maid spends a terrifying night in the adjacent bedroom. Jed, the old gamekeeper, is persuaded to tell the story of the love of two men for Kitty and the tragic events of 1825, which caused her downfall and reduced her to life in the Southwell workhouse. Eventually, the room is unlocked and the Rev. Birtwistle conducts an exorcism — but with unexpected consequences.

DR. MORELLE AND DESTINY

Ernest Dudley

Johnny Destiny, a ruthless American killer, arrives in England to blackmail a former confederate. He aims to link up with this former accomplice through the latter's daughter, Lucilla . . . Miss Frayle, Dr. Morelle's secretary, unwittingly becomes involved in the killer's quest while holidaying nearby. But Dr. Morelle learns of Miss Frayle's potential danger, and arrives at the deserted creek-side inn where they have foregathered in time to take a hand in the game . . .

A SYNONYM FOR MURDER

Robert Clarke

When Detective Inspector Eric Moran was given the Theora Folger murder case, he found it was linked to the murder of Sue Garrity, the niece of the City Treasurer of Los Angeles. Moran knew who the killer was, but needed to pin down the motive. Without that, Moran could not take the case to the City Attorney's office . . . Then, when he did find it, he also turned up another suspect who was, although he had not committed the murders, more guilty than the murderer.

THE VENTILATED HEAD

Anthony Nuttall

A pop singer, an explosive bombshell of a girl, and her hippy boyfriend. A combination like that could go any-where — or thought they could. When Matt Grant became a big time pop singer money came and went, but it went faster than it came. When the inevitable crash came, Matt worked as a door-to-door salesman — and met Lindsay. And it was then Matt found that the life of an out-of-work pop singer was more than hard — it was murder.